# DOOM'S DAY

## EXTRACTION POINT

# DOOM'S DAY

## EXTRACTION POINT

M G Harris

1

BBC Books, an imprint of Ebury Publishing
20 Vauxhall Bridge Road
London SW1V 2SA

BBC Books is part of the Penguin Random House group of companies
whose addresses can be found at global.penguinrandomhouse.com

Doctor Who is produced in Wales by Bad Wolf with BBC Studios Productions.

Executive Producers: Russell T Davies, Julie Gardner, Jane Tranter, Phil Collinson & Joel Collins

First published by BBC Books in 2023

www.penguin.co.uk

A CIP catalogue record for this book is available from the British Library

ISBN 9781785948244

Editorial director: Albert DePetrillo
Project editor: Steve Cole
Cover design: Lee Binding

Typeset in 12.5/15.5pt Albertina MT Std Pro by Jouve (UK), Milton Keynes
Printed and bound in Great Britain by Clays Ltd, Elcograf S.p.A.

The authorised representative in the EEA is Penguin Random House Ireland, Morrison Chambers, 32 Nassau Street, Dublin D02 YH68

Penguin Random House is committed to a sustainable future for our business, our readers and our planet. This book is made from Forest Stewardship Council® certified paper.

# Contents

**TWELVE HOURS**



**ELEVEN HOURS**

# Fourteen Hours

# VM2076

Doom sneaked a glance at the timer on her wrist-mounted vortex manipulator.

*Fifty-nine minutes.*

Then she'd be siphoned into the timestream to the next mission. With luck she'd finish this mission early and spend an easy ten minutes researching the next, picking from a shortlist she'd already prepared in the Lesser Order of Oberon's dispatch app. This job's location looked promising: a ski resort named 'Svoda'. Mountain resorts catered rather well to her preferred level of luxury.

Doom already felt uneasy about how little prep she'd managed for assignment VM2076, which was none, *nada*. She'd fallen well below her own standards. Most self-respecting 'knights' – or, as she preferred, 'hitters' of the Order – prided themselves on starting each fresh sixty minutes fully up to speed with relevant details. It'd been a long, stressful day and almost half of it was still left. She was desperate for a break. But if she stopped now, she probably wouldn't survive until tomorrow.

*If I do, it's two consecutive jobs from now on, absolute max.*

Every job in her app's shortlist had been flagged for signs of temporal distortion – a basic safety feature of the vortex manipulator. It was intended to warn people against visiting time-places where they might run into other time travellers. Doom was actively looking for one – 'the Doctor' – so she'd hacked it as a 'TARDIS sniffer'. As such it was rough and ready and thus far mostly good for hurling her into the timeline of time travellers that were *not* the 'Doctor' she sought. But locating a needle in a haystack meant sifting through a lot of hay. She was determined to snag any mission flagged for temporal distortion before other assassins could.

'You've done this before?' asked Mandra. The earnest young humanoid had shown up to represent Doom's client, who'd opted to remain anonymous. Two honey-brown eyes gazed out of a face with soft features, straight black hair and brown skin. Black-ink tattoos (or perhaps birthmarks) on her forehead and continuing to below her right ear were the only feature that distinguished her from trillions of 'bog-standard' humans in the known universe.

'I'm a professional,' Doom began, a little shy. It could get weird around people who knew she was there to carry out a hit. She rarely met a client and only occasionally their representative. She decided to throw back her shoulders and go with 'confidence'. 'Your boss made the right choice, going with the Lesser Order. "Where there's a kill, there's a way," we like to say.'

Mandra looked surprised. 'You're a professional skier?'

That's when Doom noticed they were standing behind a group of people wearing black or grey ski suits, all shuffling towards a counter dispensing boots, goggles, helmets and skis. She paled. Skiing? On actual snow, not virtual? It'd been a minute.

'Skiing, you say? Yeaaa ... Not a pro. More of a ... solid B.'

'The ski gear comes with haptic feedback and augmented reality. You won't need to be proficient. But your bio mentioned a job at the Jade Dragon Snow Mountain resort on Earth? I noticed you "took care" of things by arranging an unfortunate incident on the ski slopes?'

'I did, I did. Yup.'

Doom could feel the prickle of sweat beneath her collar. That particular 'unfortunate incident' had been pure luck – an accident. She'd intended to slip the target a mickey before they went speed-riding together (the target's idea) but he'd skied away rather briskly and when she'd tried to catch up, they'd collided. They'd both gone over the edge and the speed-riding wing had saved her but not him. Looked good on a bio but it wasn't something Doom had planned to repeat.

'Just out of interest, Mandra, the mountain job – your idea? Or was that your boss?'

Mandra's grin gave the game away. Not only had it been her idea, she wanted praise for it.

*Great. That's just . . . Perfect.*

Doom hated when a client tried to specify the method. Even when they didn't actually write it into a contract, they often got snippy if she didn't try it their way. Their way was usually half-baked and often not *entirely* aligned with the ethos of the Lesser Order of Oberon. She was no extremist but she had her pride. In a universe where assassination was an unfortunate necessity, the Order's principle of 'efficiently, justly, quickly' dispatching a target struck her as objectively good.

She followed as Mandra stepped up to the counter and tapped a handheld device to a console. A disembodied voice announced, 'Miz Doom, one mountain pass plus full equipment hire for the final ride of the season.'

'We have eyes on your target,' Mandra said, leading her out of the rental area to where skiers were stashing shoes in lockers and snapping their feet into boots and skis. The air was cool and fresh with a hint of something astringent.

*Not pine,* Doom thought. Tantalisingly familiar, yet strangely out of place.

'Stalgon is skiing on the glacier,' continued the client's rep. 'There's a section of woods on one side. If he takes a wrong turn there, it's an 800-metre drop.' Mandra looked expectant.

*Ohhh, I get it. 'Be impressed! Tell me how clever I am!'*

But Doom wasn't and she wouldn't. Interfering to this extent with an assassin of her calibre was both ill-mannered and wasteful. Why bother to hire a so-called knight of the Lesser Order of Oberon if you were so *very* cunning at arranging a death? With a terse smile she removed her cloak, stashed it in the backpack, exposing the sleek line of her holosuit, which she'd set to project a one-piece thermal ski outfit.

'I'll keep my shoes,' she said, stowing them on top of the cloak in the backpack. They were made of wickedly expensive, butter-soft linen-leather but even had they been grubby trainers, assassins of the Lesser Order didn't leave possessions behind.

Ten minutes to ride up the mountain leaving forty-some to find her target, Stalgon. She tucked the skis under her arm.

'Ta-ra for now,' Doom said, stepping onto a moving belt leading to the gondola.

'Sending our data to your tracker,' Mandra called out.

At the turnstile, 'Farewell Ms Doom' scrolled across the barrier. *Bit odd.* Then she remembered – the mountain pass bore her name. Just before she stepped into the packed gondola, a random skier wearing mirrored goggles and dressed like several others handed her a backpack, then disappeared into the huddle. She handled the dense bundle uncertainly. Inside was a speed-riding wing and a harness. Slinging her own kitbag round to her chest, she put on the speed-riding backpack.

The client *literally* expected her to recreate the Jade Dragon incident?

*No one tells me anything.*

# Gondola Ride

Doom flicked her monocle into position and put on the ski helmet. Tracking data displayed in her field of vision, a layer of augmented reality showing routes to Stalgon. She took another minute to put on the speed-riding harness. Not that she'd be using the client's method, probably. Unless she did. She scheduled 'a bit of a think' for a minute before the ride ended. But first – the target's geo-location data. Stalgon was riding all the way to the summit. She would intercept him from the middle gondola station. Burning precious minutes on route – but at least the views were good.

*Lovely, craggily edges. Gorgeous little log cabins.*

Seven minutes to go. Practically an eternity. Long enough to get distracted, to allow darker thoughts to intrude. The image of Death approaching in a cowl, for example.

*Don't.*

She replaced the unwelcome image with a favourite mental exercise.

*How might I kill everyone in this gondola?*

Two minutes later she was satisfied that her plan would work. She'd climb onto the top of the lift, shut both eyes so she didn't see the vertiginous drop, jam the cable mechanism, wait for the rescue vehicle while clinging on for life, open her eyes just long enough to leap across and then detonate the fission spikes she'd attached to the gondola's pulley, plunging everyone inside to their deaths.

In a just world she'd be arrested seconds later, but folk with access to a vortex manipulator didn't lose sleep about getting arrested.

She began to plan her route to Stalgon. The monocle tracker's augmented reality dovetailed nicely with the rented ski gear's haptic feedback, which was designed to let a blue slope skier like Doom cruise down black slopes. For a neophyte like her, speed-riding without haptics was essentially suicide.

The gondola came to a swinging halt. The doors slid open with a hiss. She shuffled ahead anxiously, dropped the skis to the ground, clicked into them and faced the icy snow beyond.

*Muscles, meet memory. Please?*

Doom pushed forward on her skis. The downward curve of the piste approached. Her belly felt tight, stinging with low-grade fear. Where it counted, in her legs and core, she felt only the blessed return of passable competence, thankfully. The tips of her skis had just tipped onto the downward slope when she felt something digging into the backs of her thighs. Instinctively, she turned to look; a mistake. A kid had bumped her from behind and was now pointing Doom out to their parents.

Her leading ski spun until she was sliding sideways. She tried to correct, but within seconds she'd pivoted so far that she was now careening backwards down the slope. Stunned that she was still upright, she began slowly to turn so that she could at least point the right way.

To her astonishment the child suddenly launched in pursuit, making what looked like a determined beeline for her. Two adults followed, hot on their kid's heels.

Doom bit her lip, leaned in and accelerated. The monocle tracker indicated that Stalgon had paused about a hundred metres farther down. From the distance and elevations she calculated a window of about 200 metres over which she could catch up to Stalgon and push him to a fatal fall. She could ensure it was deadly if she personally rolled him over the edge. Then she'd let go of him, spring the wing and reproduce the incident at Jade Dragon.

*Terrible method. Which bozo suggested it?*

True – the idea was flashy. There'd be kudos if Doom could pull it off. She'd have one chance to grab Stalgon and go over, one chance to engage the wing and then hold on and hope the haptics worked as well as they had that time at Jade Dragon.

*Yeaaah, it's not for me. Plan B it is.*

Doom's next thought was interrupted by an explosion of snow directly ahead. She sailed through a cloud of powder, both arms raised in an instinctive block. Her left boot took a sudden, hard blow like a kick as another cloud of snow blew up in front of her. Her mind shifted into another gear, the one she reserved for jobs categorised as 'High Risk'. This one obviously wasn't 'Medium Risk' after all.

*Target knows I'm here. Target has a fan club.*

She had to take the fan club out first – assuming she stayed upright long enough. She aimed for a thicket on the right flank of the glacier and headed for cover. The muscles of her right thigh were barely coping, shuddering with the effort of the turn.

Reaching the shelter of a tree, she drew the staser pistol from its holster and set it to stun. She spotted the kid and one parent (if that's what they were, which seemed more unlikely by the second) skiing towards the wooded flank of the piste and took aim.

A bullet slammed into a tree behind her. Flinching, she dodged behind the trunk. This contract included no bonus Conscience Payment so she'd need to avoid any collateral damage, especially the kid. But unfortunately these goons seemed to be shooting at her, although she couldn't spot a gun.

Doom sighed and pulled the trigger. 'I take no pleasure in this,' she shouted as the youngster swerved and crashed into the tree trunk.

She sensed a malevolent glare from a 'parent', even behind their goggles. They raised a gloved hand, pointing. A bullet emerged from their finger. It whizzed past her ear, splintering wood mere centimetres away.

Doom returned fire at once, then rubbed her neck where tiny splinters of wood had broken the skin. The adult skidded and slammed into the same tree.

'I take it back – I *did* enjoy it.'

She'd only stunned the kid but, even at this distance, she could see there was something badly wrong with their face. She selected the zoom function on her monocle for a closer look. She didn't want to have killed a child.

Yet where a face should have been, there was only the vacant, exposed mechanism of an android.

# ELE IN THE SKY

It'd been a dizzying five minutes since she'd exited the gondola. Stalgon was long gone, as was the possibility of rolling off the mountain with him, dropping the target like a hot brick and speed-riding gracefully into the sunset.

*That's a shame.*

Relieved, Doom started down the mountain again, skiing with caution. After a little while she was comfortable enough to take in her surroundings and even surveyed the sky. What she saw was so shocking that she veered off and almost sailed over the edge. After two minutes of exhausting, frantic course correction she calmed down enough to look up again.

She hadn't imagined it. A *mahoosive* fireball, a real-life, *freakish,* extinction-level event plummeting towards the planet. And it was definitely headed for the mountain.

*'Farewell, Ms Doom. Final ride of the season.'*

Details like that were easy to miss when you had other things on your mind, but a heads-up from Terri, her 'account manager', would have been nice.

*'You're going to love this locale; scenery to die for. Chappie by the name of Stalgon. Mind out for the planet-killing asteroid.' See how little extra effort that takes, Terri?*

A cauldron of dark emotions stirred. Was this how it ended? It was going on eleven hours since New Venice. Every moment since then felt like borrowed time.

She had no clue how the Doctor managed bumpy time dilemmas like this. She knew Time Lords existed, but until yesterday she hadn't personally encountered any. Then at the masked ball in New Venice, Doom had been introduced to a Time Lord known as 'I Doctor'. Since then she'd met two more – both turned out to be other regenerations of 'I Doctor.'

Time wasn't on Doom's side. It was a conundrum on three levels. Firstly, the relatively humdrum matter of the ticking timer on the vortex manipulator: forty-three minutes to go before she junked this entire contract – unless she killed Stalgon. Secondly, the added spice of a genocidal asteroid. *Just what this job was missing, thanks a bunch, Terri.* And thirdly, the soul-crushing, omnipresent and downright existential unpleasantness of the cowled figure that kept showing up: Death.

With a name like hers, Doom knew a walking metaphor when she saw it.

*Tick, tock, ignore the clock.*

She eyed the sky again, this time squaring up to the fearsome glare of the approaching asteroid. *Definitely getting bigger.* Which would run out of time sooner – her mission or the planet over which she now soared?

After a few more seconds she couldn't face the fireball. The tracker pinpointed Stalgon on the lowest slopes. What kind of zealot would choose to spend his last hour alive skiing? Doom wasn't planning on letting this play out much longer. She'd already let Stalgon get his kicks schussing down the mountain – that was generous enough, surely?

Plan B: she'd anticipate Stalgon at the gondola base, where an addict like that was bound to show up, lining up for one last hit. And *crackle-blam*: the satisfying sound of a lethal staser charge from her gun smacking into its target. Sincere apologies to distressed bystanders, punch out of the mission on the dispatch app and vortex along to the next job.

She spared a moment to enjoy a stunning view. The flank of mountain that *wasn't* facing a hideous, world-ending, flaming space boulder was quite lovely, really; soft rolling valleys of virgin snow, dazzling white against the stark black of tall firs and pale grey mountain cliffs. Should Doom have taken more effort to *actually* get good at winter sports?

*Too darn cold.*

She felt a twinge of sorrow for the people of this planet. Granted, she'd met only one thus far, plus two skiing androids. But Mandra seemed nice and almost certainly didn't deserve to be vaporised by an asteroid impact.

On the final run she breathed a sigh of relief. Respite

was at hand for her aching thighs. Nearing the gondola base station, she skidded to a wobbly halt just in time to avoid the swerve of a slim figure in one of the orange-and-black one-pieces worn by Svoda resort staffers. Doom was finally skiing half-decently, neat swishes that barely marked the snow. As she neared the station she pulled off her goggles.

'All right, Mandra!' she called out, relieved to see a familiar face.

Mandra turned to her blankly, no sign of recognition at first. Then something shifted in the woman's expression. Her lip curled, her nostrils flared. A snarl escaped her mouth and she raised a hand. The index finger was stretched out and aimed directly at Doom.

Doom recoiled. 'Was it something I said?' She'd fired a staser before Mandra got off a single round. 'Aw, mate. Thought we were friends. Why'd you go and become a collateral?'

While the fallen body twitched, she skied closer to examine the body. The face was frozen in glassy-eyed surprise. Feeling around the jawline, Doom found what she sought – a tiny depression. She pressed. The face came away in her hand, revealing the same inner mechanism she'd seen on the child-sized android.

'Et tu, Mandy?'

# Classic Terri

'Mandra' was apparently another of Stalgon's bodyguards. Doom guessed the client had somehow temporarily hacked this particular unit long enough to recruit its assistance and to steal tracking data.

So – this target planned to spend his final hours skiing on the very site of what would soon be a cloud of atomised rock floating above the planet, a gigantic maelstrom resembling Jupiter's eye. Android bodyguards were there to prevent anyone from stealing his precious time.

None of this had been in the briefing. Just 'Kill Stalgon, a renowned planetary systems engineer from Vassta. Coordinates and medium-level assistance supplied by client.'

*Classic Terri. Minimalist on job details, maximalist on staff satisfaction surveys.*

Targets of assassination often sniffed a threat. Many hired guards. Doom preferred to be warned in advance of possible collaterals, but clients didn't always see bodyguards as people and assumed she shared their view. She didn't. Bodyguards were no more innocent than she was, but they *were* people.

*Unless they're androids. Stalgon must be sick-rich to afford this many.*

She checked the monocle's tracker. Her target was in an ascending gondola. The next ride was loading passengers at the base. The androids she'd stasered would be back – the charge would merely scramble their systems for up to three minutes. She took another minute to survey her surroundings, shielding her gaze from the horrifying spectacle of the fireball. It was already distractingly large. She spotted three skiers on the final section of the piste. The Svoda resort was sparsely populated – Stalgon's activity of choice for his last hours didn't seem to be shared by many other inhabitants of this world.

*Don't blame them. Personally I'd sit home with a plate of peanut butter sandwiches and a giant latte and finally finish that thousand-piecer of the fiery rings of Coulabria.*

Briefly, she toyed with the idea of waiting for Stalgon to ski down again. If the target paused for a breather or to enjoy the view, Doom risked losing precious minutes. She pushed off towards the gondola base station, using the time to check the inbox on the dispatch app. As usual it was stuffed with irrelevant messages from Terri, reminders to sign a birthday card for a colleague (this particular hitter, Doom was fairly sure had been killed last month), updated risk assessment forms that had to be signed ASAP.

Something in an unread message planted her to the spot.

*ELE predicted in assignment VM2076.*

ELE? How long had that been sitting there?

*Spell it out, Terri: Extinction Level Event!* Doom had warned her handler a dozen times that she tended to scroll past three-letter acronyms. She took a breath and read the message.

*Re: assignment VM2076, target Stalgon, planetary systems engineer. An Extinction Level Event is expected in twenty-seven minutes. This is your reminder to punch out immediately on completion.*

Timed events that might occur during a mission always appeared in relative terms, since calendar dates meant little when you only ever stayed for sixty minutes. Teeth clenched, Doom checked her vortex manipulator's timer. Thirty-six minutes left on the mission, twenty-seven until the asteroid hit. She'd just lost nine minutes. After the day she'd had, this wasn't OK.

Twenty-seven minutes to oblivion? That gave her ten useless minutes in the gondola, seventeen to find and kill Stalgon. With at least three androids after her, possibly more.

*Damn-damn. Damn-damn-damn. Damn.*

If Doom had the nerve to actually use the speed-riding kit on her back, she *might* be able to catch updrafts all the way to the summit. If she were an entirely different assassin, that'd be just dandy.

Stalgon would reach the summit in roughly eight minutes. Gondolas were five minutes apart. By the time

Doom reached the mid-station, her target should be close, on his way down. There was no more time to debate. She pushed off hard, skiing towards where the gondola was taking on its final passengers and reached it just as the doors were closing.

Inside she collided with a skier, not violently enough to cause injury but local mountain etiquette was evidently strict because, as one, the entire gondola of passengers turned to face her, contempt radiating through their goggles. The skier with whom she'd collided picked herself up and removed all headgear.

Astonished, Doom whispered, 'Mandra?' There was no time to reach her weapon. She grabbed this second Mandra and picked it up, using its body to block bullets that now fired from the other passengers' fingers.

Was *everyone* at this resort an android? It actually made more sense that *only* Stalgon was obsessed enough to ski while blazing death approached. Anyone else with a sentient brain had scarpered. She'd be on her way out too, if she didn't have to finish this loser herself rather than hope the asteroid would.

*Stalgon, you utter weirdo.*

The android she used as a shield was absorbing a tirade of bullets. Two others seemed to have switched tactics, crawling below where Doom was swinging her android-shield.

*Mandra the Android: mandroid. I get it now. Ha ha, Stalgon, you're quite the wit.*

Doom dropped as low as the ski boots would allow and heaved the now-floppy body of the mandroid onto one shoulder. With one hand freed, she reached for her weapon and switched the mode to deliver a widespread electromagnetic pulse. The attacking androids now crouched low enough to shoot bullets below her shield-mandroid.

Both her ski boots cracked under fire. She triggered the wide EMP. The tech in her ski headgear went instantly dark. Doom pushed goggles away in time to see all the androids freeze as their electronics were temporarily disabled. She hurled the bullet-riddled mandroid and watched it land on top of two that had crawled towards her.

The electronics of her headgear and vortex manipulator were already resetting. After an EMP most systems could be up and running within thirty seconds, some even faster. She could shoot every one of the eight androids with a staser charge, but they'd still revive before the gondola stopped. Then what? Eight Mandra units shooting all at once was about six too many.

Maybe she could toss them out of the gondola? She tried the door. Unsurprisingly, it was locked during transit. She could use the wide EMP again after thirty seconds but then she'd have to repeat the trick all the way up. Her weapon simply wasn't designed for that, needed time to recharge after delivering each widespread EMP. Three in quick succession would probably cause the weapon to fizzle and out would come the repair kit.

Heart pounding, she stared at the timer, waiting for it to reactivate. If she'd blown it completely, she'd be trapped here *and* it'd be her own fault. She gasped with relief as it blinked back into life. An idea occurred to Doom. Maybe her idle fantasy earlier wasn't time wasted? The first half of that plan could be just the thing.

*Ridiculous idea. Downvote!*

Thirty-one minutes to go. The asteroid would hit in twenty-two.

# Stalgon's Game

Doom eyed the gondola's ceiling escape hatch. Thirty seconds left before the Stalgon fan club awakened. Just enough time to climb out. No need for fission spikes – the main thing was to get out of there. She'd use the speed-riding wing to escape. Bracing herself, she pulled her feet out of the ski boots and tried not to imagine weather conditions on top of a gondola whizzing up the mountain.

*Do. Not. Look. Down.*

Doom picked up the nearest android. It was lighter than a human, thankfully. Watery organs tended to make organic beings deceptively heavy. She ripped off its head-gear: another 'Mandra'. Doom slung it atop one that lay beneath the ceiling hatch. Heaving with effort she picked up another and dragged it on top of the first.

*Three of 'em should do it.*

Under its goggles were the exact same features, down

to what Doom recognised was almost certainly a tattoo, its geometric symmetry more obvious now that she saw the whole thing. What Stalgon had skimped on design options he'd apparently made up for in numbers. Yet only a few had attacked her. Had the first Mandra, the friendly one, conferred some kind of temporary protection while it interacted with Doom?

*Oof. Shouldn't have stopped deadlifting.*

Out of the corner of her eye she spotted one robotic hand starting to twitch. Hurriedly she clambered atop the Mandra-pile and reached for the handle on the hatch. An airlock hissed. She gripped both sides of the opening and pulled herself up, biceps burning in protest. Now she remembered why she'd quit the gym.

Doom swung her head and torso above the hatch. There was a sudden grip on her left foot. Instantly she pivoted both hips and aimed a kick. Her right foot connected with an android, dislodging it, but the other remained trapped in an unyielding grasp. With her free foot she scraped blows across her trapped ankle, trying to dislodge the thing's hand. Human fingers would have been crushed but these machines didn't let up.

She leveraged her elbows against two sides of the hatch. The android was regaining power. Doom could feel herself being stretched. Pain stabbed through both shoulder joints as the pressure increased. Gasping with effort, with two outstretched fingers she tried to reach the handle of her pistol. It was no good.

The other units would soon regain power. She thrashed about, twisting her foot until she felt its sock slacken. Another frenetic burst of energy and her foot slid out leaving the android holding the sock. With one final, desperate push, she hauled herself through the hatch and scrambled onto the top of the gondola. A stiff breeze swept her clean off the gondola and into the freezing void, hurtling into the path of a descending one.

In the shadow of the dropping gondola, she was in freefall. Eyes screwed tightly shut, she engaged the speed-riding wing. The air current might well drag her into a collision but there was nothing else she could do now. After a second she remembered to breathe gasping as her lungs ballooned with icy air.

The sound of wheels rolling on woven steel cable became louder. She felt the updraft pull on her body as the wing unfurled. It felt exactly as though she were being borne upwards, even though she knew it was merely a slower fall. Doom opened both eyes to see the falling gondola bearing down. She yanked up both knees just as it raced past.

*No. Words.*

Doom's language facilities seemed to have shut down, she was all sensation now. If skiing had been a challenge then this was light years from any comfort zone, flying high above millions of tonnes of rock, ice and snow. Both feet were bitingly cold but the left one, sockless and naked, cramped with freeze-burn. She cursed Stalgon, Mandra and the client for picking this *particular* time and this *particular* place for the hit. But after a moment she realised that the haptic feedback of the rented gear was kicking in, guiding both fingers to steer the wing.

She'd stopped trembling with terror, at least, but the

experience fell short of anything Doom considered enjoyable. She was tired of Stalgon's game.

*Staser, definitely. After this, I might even let you see it coming, you deranged jock.*

As ascending and descending gondolas receded into the distance, she began to hear a new sound: a faint, low rumble like a lion's roar. She turned her head, careful not to alter the angle of the wing, which was floating her in a gentle arc over the glacier. When she saw how much bigger the fireball had grown, she felt something she'd experienced only rarely. It was as though her internal organs were liquefying and freezing, all at once.

The last time she'd experienced this was when she'd faced the drooling, wide-jawed grin of a mutant crocodile she'd been hired to kill, the stench of whose rotten breath had reached her from ten metres away. It was a primal sensation, the ancient dread of being *prey* to a wild beast. The first time, Doom had the impression of an old, long-forgotten sensor in her brain being activated, a species memory planted millions of years before. Turned out, such a memory also existed for the approach of flaming death-by-rock from the heavens.

She began to shake, her core temperature plummeting as heat drained from her sockless foot. Thanks to the terror-from-the-sky, however, she scarcely noticed. The rock was *humongous*. Could the planet really have as much as twenty minutes left?

Ignoring the frosty burn of her left foot, Doom focused on the tracking data. Was it even reliable? After all, the mandroids appeared to be working against her. Did this client actually want Stalgon killed? Or was hiring an assassin another component of Stalgon's twisted endgame?

It wouldn't be the first time she'd been hired 'for a giggle'.

Tracking data was all she had. Moreover, not every Mandra wanted her dead – the first one had been an absolute *flirt*. Doom was sticking to her first theory: the first Mandra was either real and working for the client, or else the client had hacked that unit for her benefit. As for worrying if a client secretly wanted her dead, that was the stuff of nightmares.

*More nightmares? Fate, you're spoiling me.*

Stalgon appeared to be moving slowly, no longer downhill and *inside* the mountain. With under twenty minutes to go before they were vaporised, was her target finally showing some sign of an actual desire to survive? Could it be he had access to a deep bunker? It'd have to be pretty deep, at least one or two kilometres down. Or maybe she had a spaceship?

A horrific thought struck Doom. If she couldn't catch Stalgon, assassinate him and vortex away, she'd be stranded. That *ski-bum* was leaving her to fry.

# Ice Tunnel

In that moment it was impossible *not* to think of that creature, the shadow she called *Death*. Maybe just a shadow. Maybe a random stalker in a cowl. Or maybe she was simply getting tired, imagining things, hallucinations putting a face to her fears. For an assassin of the Lesser Order, death was always close to hand – targets could turn nasty if they caught a whiff of her intentions. But not like this. This time, Doom sensed it; *actual* death was catching up.

Death-by-rock. Death on the rocks. Scorching, blistering death. In roughly eighteen minutes and change.

Could her end be so near, hitting as she floated in thin mountain air like a flake of snow, burning her to a crisp in a tsunami of fire from the sky?

Stalgon had stopped moving. The ski gear's augmented reality gave her a close-up of the mountain where the target was located. In the sheer wall of blue ice was an opening, a square-shaped gap exactly two metres high and wide. Stalgon, according to the tracker, had stalled about twenty metres inside.

Doom felt her hopes rising. That opening was nowhere near large enough for a spaceship. There was no other opening. Stalgon had to be headed *down*. Maybe he was waiting for a ride? An elevator that plunged deep enough to protect anyone from the asteroid would take a while to reach the top. She'd once had to kill someone in a goldmine more than a kilometre underground. The elevator, dropping at terminal velocity, had taken quite a few minutes to reach the bottom.

She snapped back to her senses. *No. Impossible.* From up here she could see far in every direction – no sign of any mining facility.

The asteroid felt terrifying close. She smelt sizzling ozone and heard the crackle of atmospheric atoms being ripped apart. Yet Stalgon, that total and absolute *piece of putrid landfill*, was still playing games.

Hand quivering, she angled the wing, preparing to change direction. Glacial wind caressed her face, sent shivers through her body. Her left foot burned but she reminded herself that pain was a good sign; pain meant the nerves still worked. She held focus on the mountain, didn't look up or down and very much avoided the right-hand corner of her vision in which the asteroid blazed. She concentrated on plotting a new route, one that took her directly into the heart of the ice tunnel.

She'd have to strike a two-by-two square metre vertical target directly in the centre, not to mention releasing the speed-riding harness at precisely the right instant, or else the wing would catch a breeze and suck her right back out of the tunnel. It was a stunt that would smash even an able speed-rider to jelly and bones unless they trained for a month. Without the haptics and augmented reality of the rented gear, what Doom was about to do would be 99.9 per cent fatal. Had the anonymous client known something like this might happen? It felt like maybe they had.

The names of a few other hitters of the Lesser Order began to scroll through her mind. Haylaa. Kjaki. Loraben. They organised winter sports outings together, Doom always sent polite refusals when invited. Why hadn't one of *them* picked this crummy job?

Maybe this was how it happened. Maybe this was how Death finally caught up to her.

Doom shuddered, preparing to release the wing, the only thing that kept her from nose-diving to a jellied-bones death a thousand metres below. She wasn't suicidal. She longed for life, even with a stump instead of a foot. Life could be amazing. Guilt flickered in the wake of these thoughts. Life was good and she took that away from her targets.

*They usually deserve it. Usually.*

The wall of sheer ice was approaching fast. Her pulse raced; she heard her heart ramming against her ribs. Deep within her skull, neurons rumbled. Data streamed before her eyes as the small opening in the ice wall approached.

*Ten metres. Eight. Dammit dammit, this is it. Six. Mamacita, that's a long way down. Get ready to release. Oh, fiddles. Stalgon, I'm going to enjoy killing you.*

Two metres from the opening she felt a jolt of haptic feedback. Doom hit the emergency harness release. Behind her the wing disappeared, borne away in an instant. Tumbling, she tucked in arms and legs, making herself as compact as possible. For a second she arced, a human cannonball targeting an opening in the ice wall. Then she collided with the edge of the tunnel, head and torso slamming against the upper edge while her hips and legs swung inside. The forward momentum carried her downwards and into the opening as her hands slid down the ice. When she landed, her shoulders and head hung over the lip of the tunnel.

Doom's eyes had been tightly shut from the moment she'd hit the wall. Now she opened them slowly, shuffling her body further into the tunnel. She was staring directly up into the sky, straight into the evil eye of the asteroid. Which, she decided, she hated as much as she'd ever hated anyone or anything.

Grumbling aloud she said, 'I'd kill that asteroid for free if someone asked; that's how much I hate it.'

Once she was safely inside the ice tunnel she sat up, removed a glove and began to massage some life back into her left foot. The nerves of her frozen tissue jangled and she moaned a little, but after three minutes the sensation began to return. She wriggled her toes, whimpering with relief. Then she reached inside her one-piece suit for the shoes she'd stored, planting a kiss on each.

*Hello lovelies, bless you for being here.*

Gingerly, she put on the shoes, enjoying a rush of pleasure as each painfully tender foot was suddenly encased and protected.

The floor, walls and ceiling of the tunnel were opaque blue ice, several metres thick. It didn't feel particularly cold. Cool, definitely, but her fingertips didn't stick to any surface. *Odd.* The surface was rough, not slippery at all. She guessed some kind of maintenance vehicle swept up and down the passageways, scoring it. Shakily, she rose to her feet. She leaned back against the icy corridor and checked her timer. It was irrelevant how much time was left on the assignment's hour because the asteroid would hit even sooner. *Eight minutes before impact.*

The vortex manipulator's timer couldn't be changed but she could set a second timer, this one for time-to-impact. In the relative safety of a place where she could stand and walk on solid ground, she took six calming breaths before she checked the monocle's tracker.

Stalgon was close!

# COLLIDE

Doom limped deeper into the tunnel. Her target was still thirty metres away but at least on the same level. Ahead the tunnel joined another passageway that crossed it lengthways. Stalgon was pretty much stationary, somewhere to the right. As Doom neared the junction, she heard a metallic rumble. The crunch of gears and heavy machinery turning. To her horror, a vehicle appeared ahead, backing up, turning in from the crossing passageway and advancing slowly into the exit tunnel.

She glanced backwards, even though she knew nothing had changed. There was still only one way in or out. The tunnel-tram was grinding towards her, still reversing. She began to wave her arms in wild, expansive gestures. Surely they had a rear-view mirror?

'Hey! I'm in here! Halt! Ahoy there! Stop!'

But it didn't stop. The tunnel-tram just kept coming, like some grotesque syringe plunger bearing down on her, preparing to expel her from the side of the mountain as if she were half a mill of vaccine. If she turned and ran, she might avoid being crushed but without the speed-riding wing she'd fall and *jellybones.*

So she did the opposite. Pelted towards the tram as it backed slowly towards her and leapt onboard, grasping at a doorhandle. Its D-bar was sturdy enough to take her weight, but the tram didn't stop backing up. Doom pressed her face against the glass and held on as the vehicle pushed on towards the open end of the tunnel. Inside the cabin were four passengers.

*Mandra and her three identical quadruplets.*

The mandroids regarded her with bland disinterest. After a brief, curious look they ignored her, ignored the fact that the tram was apparently on its way off the side of a mountain.

Doom wanted to scream with frustration. They hadn't yet identified her as a threat – maybe she could get inside, dash through the tram and out the other end before it hurtled to disaster? She pulled open the door and squeezed through the gap.

Once inside, she didn't stop to watch their reaction. She sprinted down the narrow walkway past the seated androids. She skipped over the legs of the first, groaning as her frostbitten left foot crashed to the floor. She was preparing to leap over the second when the unit rose suddenly and held out an arm. Doom crashed into it and was thrown back but remained standing. She reached for her weapon but the nearest android struck the pistol out of her hand. Then it grabbed her by the shoulders and threw her backwards into the arms of the first unit she'd passed. It wrapped both arms around Doom in a crushing embrace. The pleasant features of the bodyguard who faced her were now twisted into a grimace.

'Mandra,' she stammered. 'Fancy meeting you up here.'

The unit delivered a stinging slap to her cheek. 'Be quiet. What do you want with Stalgon?'

'What do *I* want? You're the one who told me to track him!'

The units were almost certainly networked, sharing memories. Doom's client either owned or had hacked at least one, which meant that the anonymous client might still have access to the system. Her only hope now was that they might once again intervene, if she could buy some time.

She continued in the same indignant tone. 'There's an asteroid on its way, you know that don't you?'

'Why do you seek Stalgon?'

Doom pretended not to hear. 'And this tram? It's backing out of a tunnel into nothingness. Literal air and a thousand-metre drop. Quite a bit more, if I'm honest, but it's the first thousand metres that worry me.'

The unit struck her other cheek. 'Shut up. Who sent you?'

With both arms firmly pinned by the mandroid behind her, Doom could only wince. 'Tell you what, let's hurry up out of here and I'll . . .'

She paused. The tram had stopped moving. The other two bodyguards stood and began to approach. Their expressions were, she decided, as unpleasant as any she'd yet seen. One picked up and pored over her discarded weapon.

'That asteroid,' Doom insisted. 'It's going to crash into this mountain pretty soon. I think your mate Stalgon might want to worry about *that* a bit more than little old me.'

The nearest android peered at her for several seconds as if trying to read her expression. 'We know,' it said, very matter-of-fact. 'Stalgon is leaving soon.'

'Oh, nice. Got a ship has he? A lil' tiny ship, whoosh him off mountain?'

The unit fixed her with a determined glare. 'You will tell us who sent you.'

'I would gladly tell you,' Doom replied. 'Thing of it is, though, I don't actually know.'

Mandra looked neither convinced nor concerned. 'Then you'll die.'

Doom was silent. Odds were, she'd die anyway. Yet they must actually care about the answer to their question or else by now she'd be dead. What was next, torture?

*Better get on with it; it's flaming-Mandra time in about four minutes.*

The mandroid holding on to her suddenly swung her around for a complete one-eighty. Doom felt the hard poke of a gun pressed to the back of her head. A sharp kick to a hamstring followed, and a shove. 'Move.'

She looked ahead, suddenly understanding what they planned. The end of the tram was bathed in blue-white light. It was poking out of the end of the tunnel. Beyond was only freezing air and a deadly fall.

Panic gripped, and Doom dug in her heels. 'No. Wait. Seriously. You need to get off this world. I know you're mechanoids but you must have some programming for self-preservation. Right? You're not going to let Stalgon force you to stay here to be roasted, are you? Cos that's what'll happen. Oh yeah, it's not just organic life forms that die from a thing like this. You might go even sooner, if the atmosphere catches fire before the asteroid lands. Oh, it's a *scene*. Y'know, from a *very* long distance.'

The mandroids didn't shoot, but they did get behind Doom to push and keep pushing until she'd been forced into a stumbling death march headed for the tunnel's opening. One android climbed over seats to bypass her and pushed open the rear door. A frozen gust whipped through the tram. The dull roar of the asteroid was unmistakeable now, could not be dismissed as imagination or background noise. She shut her eyes as the android shoved her to the brink.

'Who sent you?'

How could Stalgon not know? Doom shook her head, refusing to face the void. 'If you've figured out enough to hire bodyguards, you tend to have some clue.'

No one answered. She opened one eye warily then, in astonishment, both. Something inexplicable was happening in the sky. A spacecraft had emerged from behind the corona of the fireball and was now clearly visible, dazzling as it reflected the full glint of the sun. It appeared to be speeding directly into the heart of the fireball.

Doom boggled at the spectacle. There could only be seconds before impact. Then what? It was too late to divert the asteroid, which was the usual way these things were managed. The alternative – smashing the giant rock this close to a planet – would cause dozens of smaller impacts all over the world, some of which could be almost as lethal as the big one.

'Mandy, please, I'm begging you, can we talk about this—'

She broke off. It was happening, right before their eyes. The spacecraft entered the corona. The asteroid wobbled. In slow motion it appeared to break into several large chunks. The pieces fell away and, *exactly* like some breath-taking firework display performed impossibly high, each set off on its own fiery trajectory. Not a single one was headed for the mountain.

# ACQUISITION

There was something very wrong with the mandroids. The arms that had gripped her like a vice relaxed and when Doom shucked herself free, didn't resist. She stepped back and with a swift heave, shoved one gawping unit through the open door of the tunnel-tram and over the side of the mountain. It fell in total silence. The others didn't respond, their eyes still fixed on a sky now filled with dozens of trails of fire streaking across the sky, carrying chunks of the asteroid in every direction.

Doom watched for a moment, bemused, then snatched her pistol out of the hand of the unit that'd picked it up. She was tempted to wait a few seconds more to see if the mandroids snapped out of their reverie, but it seemed risky – so she shot a charge into all three then dragged the motionless units out of the tram and over the edge. Only one remained, out of reach and apparently no longer interested in her.

She pointed her weapon. 'Hey, Mandra. Why the change of heart?'

The android turned to her. 'Who sent you?'

'Huh. Is it weird that I thought we were past that?'

The unit raised its arm abruptly, gun-finger outstretched, but Doom fired first; two zaps to the head. She couldn't risk it reviving so she dragged the unit to the door and booted it off the edge of the mountain. Then she checked the monocle. Stalgon was on the move again, descending.

She began to run; through the tram and out of the front door of the single cabin, down the tunnel and to the junction, switching right and to where she realised Stalgon had been waiting, a viewing platform in the side of the mountain. Beyond were the elevators. She noticed that one had descended to one level below. She was heading for the stairs so that her target didn't realise she was moving in, then stopped. According to the tracker her target was now seventy metres below.

Doom understood at once; so much rock between levels was absolutely necessary for a spacecraft bunker. She'd been right – her target was planning to fly out. The augmented reality map of the mountain had shown no other openings. Could Stalgon have access to the AR data, had he hidden his escape route?

The idea alone was deeply disturbing. Stalgon having access to an augmented reality gave him every possible advantage. For all Doom knew, she was tracking a ghost in the machine.

She checked the vortex manipulator timer – ten minutes left on job VM2076. She had neither the time nor the energy to waste scurrying downstairs. She waved her hand over the elevator sensor, summoning a ride. When the doors opened on Stalgon's level Doom pressed herself against one side of the elevator, weapon drawn. But the target wasn't lurking in the obvious place to kill her. Nor did there seem to be any android bodyguards here. The elevator led to a rock tunnel that opened out some ten metres ahead, a flood-lit area that she guessed was the launch bay.

Maybe Stalgon wasn't even aware of her presence? Had the mandroids been programmed to interrogate or destroy anyone or anything that tried to interfere during the last minutes of the asteroid's descent? It'd explain why their killy ways had ceased the instant the asteroid had broken up and why the units had lost interest in her once they'd seen it destroyed.

It was tempting to relax but she had a bad feeling. Something about this place had felt off from the start, right from the weird smell. *Bergamot, that's it! Not pine; bergamot.* Now she'd started to doubt her eyes, too.

Surprising the target offered Doom several options. She could sabotage the escape ship. She could shut the launch bay doors on it. Both methods were a tad violent but a step up from *crackle-blam*. She crept along the corridor, keeping to the shadier side. Close to the launch bay she heard footsteps and occasional statements from what sounded like a belligerent alien voice speaking over a loud comms system.

*'The design was exactly as specified, Stalgon.'*

And, *'There can be no question of a refund.'*

And, *'No, that's not what we agreed. We suggest you examine your contract.'*

Doom entered a launch bay that was around twenty

metres high by thirty metres wide. At one side a four-person interplanetary skiff stood in the mouth of a launch tube. She guessed they were deep into the mountain because no natural light reached inside. Through the launch tube she heard a low, distant boom. Seconds later the whole room shuddered, briefly. The first and hopefully nearest of the asteroid fragments had landed.

A tall humanoid with similar skin and hair to the mandroids but no tattoo stood facing away from her and before a giant screen. Doom squinted at the tracker. She'd found Stalgon.

'You've destroyed my experiment!' railed Stalgon, all his attention on the screen in front of him. 'Of course we want a refund!'

Stalgon's interlocutor was an alien from a species she didn't recognise with leathery, grey-green skin, a vaguely lizard-like appearance and an unfortunately morose resting-face. It sounded deeply affronted and indignant. Doom was tempted to see how this played out, but she was hungry and getting tired. Less than nine minutes before she was vortexed away; just enough time to grab coffee and a bite to eat and to cast an eye over instructions for the next job.

She paused. The staser blast was quick but *so* dull, especially compared to the elegant sky-struggle she'd envisaged at the start of the hour.

*Efficient? Yep. Just? Definitely. Quick? Oh yes sir, so quick.*

Her stomach rumbled. *Crackle-blam it is, then.*

Stalgon went down like a sack of potatoes, hadn't even seen it coming. The alien observing via the comms link, however, emitted an outraged squeal.

*'I saw that! Murderer!'*

Doom fired four times into the console. The screen went dead. She checked her timer. Just enough time for a badly needed snack while she scanned through her shortlist of jobs. The only way she knew how to avoid her shadow-stalker was not to hang around more than the hour. Which had been OK-ish for the first ten hours. Now it was getting irritating.

'Where'd you keep the biscuits, Stal?'

She opened drawers randomly. No biscuits. She peered around the bay, sniffing for pastry. In one corner stood a metal closet. Approaching, she practically smacked into a man who'd suddenly rounded the corner. The monocle tracker had given her zero warning of his approach. It was as though he'd appeared from – well, from what appeared to be a dead end, just beyond the closer.

A new sound began to reverberate around the launch bay. It echoed and pulsed, growing in power and volume. Something was materialising inside the bay. Doom raised her pistol as its outline solidified. It was a blue box, taller than an above-average human and wide enough to fit four people, maybe six if they bunched up. When the door opened, she slowly backed away.

A human male in his forties stepped aside, jauntily. 'Hey, you all right?'

He was tall and slim and wore a short black leather coat the style of which Doom hadn't seen for centuries. Either this guy was seriously into vintage or else here, finally, was the time traveller her vortex manipulator had detected.

She straightened her shoulders. 'Bit late, aren't you?'

# Nine

The instant the man saw Doom he grinned. 'Hello! Miz Doom, isn't it?' He took a few strides before noticing the prone body of Stalgon on the floor. 'Oh dear, you two have a disagreement?'

Doom holstered her weapon. 'No. I killed him. He was my target. Quick question – have we met?'

'Course we have, I'm the Doctor.' A frown flickered over his face. 'Time travel can be like finding a diary of your early life – you remember parts of the story but not the peripherals. Nice to meet you, peripheral! Did I not mention I might look different next time?

For a moment she struggled to make sense of what he'd just said and then decided to save time and just ignore the bits she didn't understand. 'The Doctor, right. You look. . . . Huh. How can I put it nicely?'

'Younger?' He chuckled.

'Younger?' She swallowed. 'One way of putting it. Another would be "like another person."'

But the Doctor had apparently already lost interest, instead searching the clothing on Stalgon's corpse.

'Hey, isn't that a bit dodge . . . ?'

Ignoring Doom, the Doctor headed for the console that still crackled from the damage her weapon had inflicted. He pointed an accusing finger at the smouldering comms screen. 'This you, too?' Disapprovingly, he shook his head then set about examining the console. He evidently found whatever it was, kneeled down and inserted a key he'd taken from Stalgon's pocket.

Doom sighed. Her left foot burned, her muscles ached and she hadn't found the biscuits.

*When will I learn? You* always *carry pastry.*

But the Doctor was here and she had questions. She was almost out of time, and the Doctor didn't seem all that keen to make any for her.

From the console the Doctor plucked what appeared to be a data storage stick. He pocketed it, got to his feet and waggled a finger at Doom.

'Dangerous career, yours. Messy job on the asteroid, by the way. Normally my responsibility, saving people and that. Although there's something weird about this set-up, have you noticed? This system doesn't have an asteroid belt. The odds against one coming here are extremely-stupidly-stupid to one. Must admit I was a bit surprised when I got the alert. Between you and me it was already too late. The credit's all yours, pal.'

'Nothing to do with me. Look, lovely to see you and all, but I'm in a bit of a pickle and I don't have a lot of time. Got a minute?'

'I hope they paid you well, whoever it was. Cos I imagine there'll be a few people pretty angry with how this turned out. Wouldn't want you to be the one they blamed.'

Doom was so bewildered that she briefly forgot her existential situation. 'Angry that their world isn't going to be destroyed? Is that a joke?'

'They didn't think it was going to be destroyed,' he said, apparently indifferent. 'That was sort of the point. In fact they might even argue that what's happened is worse than what they predicted.'

Doom checked her assignment timer. Three minutes left. She had to research the next job, she *had* to. Lack of research had almost made this one her last.

'This all started on New Venice,' she blurted. 'A few minutes after I first met you. Did you know?'

The Doctor looked momentarily confused. 'New Venice? Oh, yeah. That's right, at the masked ball. I almost forgot about that time.'

Now *Doom* was confused. 'About *that* time . . .?' What was he trying to say?

'That time, this time. Time's circular, some say, d'you ever hear that?'

He was being evasive. She resolved not to be evaded. 'You were there, Doctor, if that's really you. *Another* you, I mean. You saw what happened – you *must* have!'

'Well . . . I see a lot of things.' He sounded deliberately vague.

'C'mon, man, help out a fellow time traveller.'

The Doctor looked pensive. 'Yeah, thing is, that *other* me wouldn't appreciate *this* me getting involved. But – not going to lie; ontologically speaking, it doesn't look good.'

'Ontologically? No kidding! You saw what happened! My question is – *how* am I still alive?'

The Doctor stood back a little, regarding her with sympathy. His silence seemed to confirm Doom's fears.

'I'm not going to be alive for much longer, am I?'

The Doctor grimaced. 'I'm sorry.'

Doom took a breath. The timer was counting down: 140 seconds. 'Dammit. Can't talk now, I need to move on. It's coming for me. I need to find the *you* I met at the ball before, well, y'know.'

She flipped open the vortex manipulator's case. In the location field of the job shortlist her eye caught a mention of 'Satellite Five'. The dining there was famously magnificent. The mission was to kill an 'ethereal'. Ethereal existence was always a hot conversation topic at parties. The set-up sounded odd enough to attract the Doctor, a notorious magnet for 'weird'. She signed the contract and waited for the transaction to be approved.

The Doctor offered a hand. 'Strange profession, if you don't mind me saying.'

'No, you're fine. It's a living,' Doom replied, more wearily than she'd usually say it. 'Maybe what's happening is for the best.'

'You don't really believe that. But maybe you should.'

The Doctor's unexpected display of empathy was weirdly disconcerting. Doom gestured at her vortex manipulator and the Lesser Order's dispatch app. 'So I'm just going to get on with . . .'

'No problem, leave you to it. Only . . . can I ask? Aren't you curious about this place?'

'Sure,' Doom agreed, with a polite smile. 'It's just, I'm . . .'

'Busy.' The Doctor tipped his forelock. 'Got it. Don't mind me.' He paused. 'Before I landed, I intercepted a communication into this console. Any chance you saw who it came from?'

'Actually, yes. Non-humanoid. Leathery skin, sort of greyish-green. Face like a disappointed handbag. Most insistent about not giving my target a refund for something.'

The Doctor beamed. 'Sounds about right! A Kraal.' He gave an expansive wave of his hands. 'Then this is a Kraal simulation, all of it.'

Doom swayed. 'This is . . . a virtual reality simulation?'

'Nothing virtual about it! That's the beauty of a Kraal simulation, it's all physical. Verisimilitude is their USP. This'll be some carefully selected, uninhabited planet, almost entirely populated with pretty realistic androids. Probably created an atmosphere bubble over the active zone. Imagine they'll have lugged the asteroid here, too, because, like I said, there's no asteroid belt in this system.'

She thought about the ice tunnel that wasn't icy, the pines that smelt of bergamot. Only those details had seemed wrong, otherwise it felt 100 per cent real; the mountain air, the cold, the snow, the earnest expressions of the mandroids.

'Hang on,' she said, puzzled. 'Did you just say there's no asteroid belt in this system?'

The Doctor gave a knowing nod. 'Yeah. Interesting, that.'

Doom frowned. 'Why go to all this trouble to destroy a random planet with an asteroid?'

The vortex manipulator didn't leave her to hear the answer.

# Thirteen Hours

# Karaoke

'Large latte, extra shot, Icelandic oat milk.'

The machine began to spurt her order into a glass. Doom picked up the finished drink. A number '5' had been drizzled onto its creamy foam head. She stood in the antechamber of a deck on what appeared to be a space station or deep underground. Ventilation pipes ran along each flank of the deck and there was a giant number '333' on the tallest wall. From behind the sliding doors to the main deck came raucous sounds and glimpses of a razzle-dazzle light show.

*Party mode on.*

Sipping her latte, Doom headed for the music. As she stepped onto the main deck a roaming blue spotlight moved past her and then rotated back. When it stopped directly overhead, the gathered crowd broke into cheers. A second later a sturdy lollipop microphone had been pushed into her hands by a young woman dressed in a flouncy, turquoise party dress, who was beaming at her, eyes brimming with encouragement. Doom's ears rang with the sound of laughter and pleading.

'Sing! Sing! It chose yoouuuu!'

Doom's trembling fingers closed around the mic. She coughed slightly. 'Honestly, it's been ages . . .'

'Siiiing!'

Nervously, she cleared her throat. The instant she'd accepted the mic, song titles were projected into the air. Silence fell gradually as she touched a finger to the 'Classics' section – it seemed like a safer bet for a citizen of the (very likely) ancient 52nd century, like Doom. 'Let It Go'. 'Problems Like These'. 'To All Catkind'.

She kept scrolling. A quick song was doable, wasn't it? She didn't even know what the next target looked like, anyway, not yet. Ten seconds later she still couldn't choose.

'Oooh. So tense!' The woman who'd handed her the mic hissed through teeth gritted in a rigid smile. 'Just pick one. Anything.'

'Mind's gone blank . . .' Doom whispered.

'Touch the blue sensor on the mic. It uses sensory feedback to limit the list to songs you know *really* well.'

From a vastly reduced list she picked 'It Had To Be You'. The piano introduction began. Doom's heart pounded. With one hand she gripped the edge of her cloak. Excitement and anticipation hit so hard that she felt faint. *How* had she forgotten this incredible sensation? She felt her chest swelling as she gripped the mic.

*'Why do I do just as you*
*Why must I just give you your way*
*Why do I sigh*
*Why don't I try to forget*
*It must have been that something lovers call fate*
*Kept on saying I had to wait*
*I saw them all*
*Just couldn't fall 'til we met'*

When the song was over, the audience burst into delighted applause. A tall guy in a sateen, white-and-turquoise suit plucked the microphone out of Doom's hand.

'Only one hour until she arrives,' he crooned. 'Are you ready, Satellite Five? Are you ready to party with Cathica?'

A huge roar went up and the blue spotlight began a new journey as the crowd clapped along with the rhythm.

Doom was still buzzing as she stumbled through the crowd and towards tables at the rear of the deck, where a handful of people milled around tables of snack food and a drinks machine. This suited her fine – she'd intended to start this hour by addressing her most urgent need: coffee. *Then* research. She'd somehow lost her latte in the karaoke crowd, so she lined up to collect another. She tried to check the monocle's screen.

The monocle was gone, too. It must have fallen. She dropped to her knees immediately, hunting it out.

'I'm not one for hyperbole,' murmured a voice above

her. 'You were – and bear in mind I'm holding back – *unbelievable*.'

Panicking slightly, Doom stood up. Searching her pockets, she turned to see that the woman in turquoise had followed. Flustered, she replied, 'Oh, thanks. I chose an easy song.'

'There are no easy songs. Are you a professional?'

Doom laughed at the irony. All the alternative career options were cropping up today. 'Me? Nah. I just love the classics.'

'Me too. Adore. Did you know, it's thanks to Cathica that one of the Empress's first decrees was to improve the quality of entertainment throughout the empire? The Jagrafess had us eating junk and watching pure trash.'

'Uh-huh,' Doom agreed, increasingly anxious about her missing monocle. She'd never heard of the 'Jagrafess'. Definitely the *future*, then. Hopefully Earth still existed.

'Are you OK?' asked the woman as Doom sank to her knees, patting the carpet in search of the monocle. 'Lost a contact lens?'

Doom forced a smile. 'Something like that, yeah.'

'Why bother with lenses when there's surgery? There's a free clinic on the station – they'll sort you out in five minutes. Or go with glasses, they'd suit you. Get white frames to match your eyeliner.'

'Yup.' Turquoise Dress had just edged out of the 'entertaining' category and into 'time-waster'.

*No monocle? Fine, I'll old-school it.*

Without the tracker, she'd have to guess what the target looked like, as Terri rarely bothered with a written description. She scanned the area, wondering vaguely if there were any data-points she could use to access public information. In the centre of the lounge stood a brass plinth on which was mounted a sculpture, an impression of a human hand.

From behind she heard a child's voice speak into the drinks machine. 'Horchata.' He was around nine or ten, a human boy, brown skin, light brown eyes and short black hair and wore what Doom decided was either a school uniform or fancy dress; a maroon-coloured one-piece under a fitted, charcoal-grey bomber jacket. The right upper arm displayed an insignia in silver thread.

She grunted, waiting for the karaoke fan to tell the kid off for queue-jumping. The young boy merely peered at her, initially puzzled and then annoyed.

'Da, there's a strange lady stopping me getting my drink.'

'Me? No, no!' Doom turned around, hoping the woman in turquoise might defend her. But she'd gone.

She handed the kid the frothy white drink. 'Sorry kiddo, I thought that other lady was ahead of you.'

The boy took the drink, frowned and walked off. Doom called after him, 'I see manners aren't what they were.'

The thrill of performance hadn't worn off yet. It had thrown her entirely. She remembered little of the mission other than something about killing an ethereal. Most important was the proximity of a time-distortion. Somewhere on the station was a time traveller – hopefully, the Doctor she was looking for, or at least a different one, one who'd be willing to help. Hopefully *not* some other kind of time traveller. On the whole, they were a pain.

From the joyous cheering, Doom guessed that the next karaoke 'volunteer' had been found. It was time to leave, find somewhere quiet where she could study her mission brief.

*Assignment VS3032. Kill ethereal being on Satellite Five, Year 200,003. Ethereal will initiate contact.*

*Is that all? Literally, classic Terri.*

Doom assumed Terri meant 'ethereal' in its euphemistic sense. The indelicate version was 'ghost', although it wasn't always considered polite to mention *any* state of post-material-death. The Lesser Order preferred to think of themselves as 'death-positive'. When your business entailed the *removal* of a pre-material-death state of being, it made sense to be candid about the post-death state, too.

Another anonymous client. At least this one hadn't sent a representative to hint at their preferred method of assassination. On the other hand, in this case she would have welcomed some guidance. How the heck did you kill a 'ghost'?

Doom wandered over to the nearest information terminal and positioned her hand.

'Direct transmission to mind-port no longer available. Kindly select your instructor's avatar,' intoned a pleasingly soft-spoken, gender-neutral voice. A range of options appeared. Doom selected 'Professor Yoon', who presented as a ten-centimetre hologram of an elegant

Korean woman dressed in a tailored pink suit and reminded her vaguely of a favourite teacher at her middle school.

'Professor Yoon, how do I kill a ghost?'

'Ethereals occupy material space within a certain density range. While you and other extant beings exist in normal material space, an ethereal cannot coincide in the same plane of existence unless these density conditions are met, or else their photonic structure loses coherence.'

'Huh. Interesting. What are the extremes of this range?'

'Hello again!' The woman in turquoise approached from behind and dropped herself casually into a nearby easy chair. 'Hope I'm not interrupting?'

Doom stared for a second until she recovered her manners. She was about to withdraw her hand from the terminal when the woman leaned forward.

'It's my first audience with the Director of Satellite Five,' the woman admitted. 'I'm actually a bit nervous. I mean, we owe Cathica so much, don't we? How about you?'

Doom responded with a bland smile. The woman had settled in as though she expected to spend the next few minutes or longer there. She had a pleasant face, fresh complexion, chestnut hair and blue eyes. She looked around thirty years old but surgery and chemicals could easily double that.

*Am I being chatted up?*

Just in case, Doom prepared herself to deliver lines she'd so often used before to let down gently anyone that tried to befriend her while she was working. 'Look,' she began, with a rueful smile. 'You seem awfully nice—'

'But you're here on business,' the woman interjected with effortless poise.

Doom leaned back in her seat, nonplussed.

'You don't have long,' continued the stranger, 'but you wish you had. We'd probably be friends under different circumstances. You *would* take my contact details but you're not from around here and you don't know when you'll be back.'

'Wow,' Doom chuckled. 'Smooth, but not too much. Like it.'

# *GHOST V WHATEVER*

The woman in the turquoise gown smiled, suddenly a little shy, almost bashful. 'How did I do, fifty per cent? More?'

It was charming. Doom couldn't hold back a smile. 'Like, eighty-five. Love the "don't know when you'll be back" bit. Mind if I steal it?'

The woman nodded graciously. 'Be my guest.' There was an awkward pause. With a soft laugh she stood up. 'You like me more already. But you still have to work.'

'Oh, you're *good*.'

The woman batted her eyes. 'Oh, I *know*.'

Doom flinched as an unseen finger jabbed her shoulder. Irritated, she whipped around to see the kid again, who asked, 'Why do you keeping talking to yourself?'

She wafted him away. 'Mind your own business, nosey.'

Doom turned back to the woman in turquoise but

once again, the elusive figure was gone. She checked the vortex manipulator's timer. Forty-nine minutes. After the latest gruelling hour in Stalgon's simulation, she wasn't feeling super-committed about this mission. Assassinate a *ghost*? She carefully read the header on the dispatch app.

*Yep, it really says that. Mad as I thought.*

There was no honour lost in failing to assassinate a ghost, she decided. She'd never heard of it being done, on the other hand. There'd definitely be kudos. For any hitter with a future, it was quite the opportunity. But that wasn't Doom; not unless she found the Doctor, the real Doctor, the one she'd met on New Venice.

Despite the Doctor-in-leather-coat's gloomster response, she refused to believe that a Time Lord couldn't help with her apparent lack of a future. And yet all the Doctors she'd stumbled upon in the past half-day were offering her nothing. She had to believe that, eventually, she'd find one who *would*.

Her most recent encounter with the Doctor had been cut short; very irritating. In the heat of the moment, she hadn't even stopped to wonder why a Time Lord would show up to save a simulation. She'd seen no actual people on the Kraal's fake-Vassta, only Stalgon. All that effort to save one non-exemplary humanoid? It was a bit much. Not even the Doctor had seemed particularly bothered to find the engineer dead.

The more she thought about it, the more irked she became. She'd wasted a chance to ask the Doctor how to contact that other incarnation, the 'Doctor' she'd talked to at the masked ball. Hadn't even bothered to ask what he was doing in the Kraal simulation. He'd been visibly tampering with some component of the simulation's console. Had the Doctor grabbed the data core?

*What's it to him?*

Glancing around, she noticed a diverse smattering of well-dressed aliens among the humans. The year 200,003 was as far into the future as she'd ever been flung. Fine dining, karaoke and multiculturalism seemed to be thriving on Satellite Five. Earth itself, however, might be a burnt husk by now, for all she knew. Doom hoped it wasn't. If humanity, with all its recklessness and violence, had a future, there might be hope for her, too.

She ambled over to an information port and resumed the dialogue with 'Professor Yoon'.

'To destroy an ethereal, it is necessary to compromise the spatial distribution of their photons,' continued the distinguished avatar, until someone interrupted.

'Killing a ghost, eh? Been there, done that.'

Doom looked up. Standing over her was a human man. Middle-aged, he had on a hip-length, crisp white, frilly shirt over a sage-coloured kilt and, draped over his shoulders, a terracotta-coloured cashmere sweater.

*Pirate shirt with cashmere? That's bold.*

He'd obviously been eavesdropping whilst tucking into a huge piece of chocolate cake. Cake in hand, he offered a fist-bump.

'Loved the performance, by the way,' he commented in a languid voice. 'Gorgeous voice.'

Doom returned the bump and ignored the compliment. 'You've killed a ghost? When? How?'

'Oh, not me. I merely produced the show. Quite the

hit.' The man allowed himself a brief smile. 'Do you have an agent?'

'Why?'

'Our show – you might find it interesting.'

'The one with the ghost-killing?' Doom replied, cautiously. Side-tracking could be a risk if you struck up a conversation during a job. This guy, however, might prove useful. A crib-sheet for this unusual challenge was tempting.

The man surveyed the area then perched on a nearby barstool. 'Andre Kulekvo, at your service. I'm a television producer. Documentaries, high-end content. You're a time traveller, aren't you?'

This could be dangerous. Only the Doctor and other hitters she'd met had ever clocked Doom as a time traveller. The producer pointed discreetly to the vortex manipulator on her wrist. He lowered his voice. 'Not my first rodeo with one of you. Are you in the Lesser Order of Oberon, too?'

Doom hesitated. Her cover wasn't necessarily blown – the producer might be part of her client's *mise-en-place*. 'Tell me more. About the ghost, I mean.'

'I'll tell you everything. *If* you promise to let me record it. Good sport that you evidently are, should be fun, no?'

'Record what, me killing a ghost? It'd have to be in the next forty-five minutes, give or take.'

Kulekvo looked pleased. 'I'm so glad we understand each other. And – I didn't catch your name?'

Doom checked her timer. The seven minutes she'd allotted for rest and recreation were gone. She eyed his cake. 'Better eat up. And it's Doom, just Doom. Not Just-Doom, just . . . Doom, yeah?'

A minute later they were strolling the corridors of Satellite Five headed for the producer's studio.

'Love the moniker. Our series goes by *Ghost v Whatever*. The concept is: we recruit volunteers to encounter ghosts. Usually it's some former acquaintance, a business rival, an old lover, that sort of affair. There's always something unresolved, obviously it's all about the closure.' Kulekvo paused and continued more delicately. 'Occasionally the closure they seek is *terminal*. Our "whatever" desires to end a person's post-death existence.'

'What do you want with me?'

Kulekvo clasped his hands. 'You're a professional assassin, yes?' In an aside he whispered, 'A – let's call them an "acquaintance" – of mine sported a bracelet just like yours. Shan't disclose their name, for obvious reasons.'

Doom stopped walking. 'You made a show where an assassin kills a ghost?'

'Not yet – that would be your contribution: *Ghost v Assassin*.'

'Why would anyone want to kill a ghost? They're just projections.'

'Don't be so hasty; allow me to give you a for-example. Take our last show – *Ghost v Parent*. An individual had deeply, *deeply* wronged their son, you see, and our client had seen to it that the villain ended their days in prison. But when our client heard their nemesis had opted for Corinthian resurrection, well, they weren't exactly thrilled. And they came to us.'

Doom had heard of Corinth Inc. – the company had pioneered a service offering post-life existence as an ethereal. Clients could choose to exist in a non-corporeal form based on a persona synthesised from their biography and communications data. Like many others, Doom personally didn't consider this a true continuation of life, but apparently it could be of comfort to the bereaved. Although obviously *not* to the parent of someone the ghost had harmed in their material life.

'Guarantee the method and location and you're on. But seriously, chop-chop.'

Kulekvo nudged her. 'Oh yes, I know all about you knight-assassins and your "killing hour". That's how my honey referred to it. Now – I wonder if there's any way to include that *darling* voice of yours in the show.'

Doom blanched. *My 'honey'? Yikes.*

# ENGAGEMENT

'To kill a ghost you must first catch a ghost,' the producer declared, with a hint of grandiosity. 'And to catch a ghost you must first lure it.'

'That's the easy bit. According to my mission brief, this ghost is supposed to make contact with me.'

Kulekvo looked delighted. 'Any idea when? I only ask because you did seem *somewhat* preoccupied with time.'

Doom gave him a crafty smile. 'Oh, it already has.'

'Really? Do tell.'

It'd taken a few minutes to put the obvious together but, now that she had, Doom wanted to share how clever she'd been. 'We're looking for a human woman dressed in a mid-length turquoise gown, a bit flouncy and worn off one shoulder. I'd guess she's around thirty years old, dark brown hair, pinkish skin, no obvious tattoos, blue eyes, medium height.'

'Excellent,' quipped the producer. 'Narrows it down

considerably – turquoise is the colour of the entertainment staffers on Satellite Five. And you know this female is your ghost, exactly how?'

'She's a teeny bit obsessed with me. It happens, with some targets. She keeps disappearing on me.' Doom paused, thinking of the young boy's bewilderment when she'd mentioned the woman. 'And other people can't see her.'

'That's grand! We'll configure the cameras to detect a ghost by that description. Ghosts are only visible to designated hauntees but they can't fool our cameras. In the meantime, wait here a jiffy, I'll nip off and set everything up.'

Doom tapped her vortex manipulator. 'Forty-eight minutes before I vortex out.'

'It'll take me about twenty to set everything up. The studio is right here on Satellite Five. Terribly clever – we can conjure any manner of haunted house! Looks absolutely genuine and you won't have to step off the station. All *you* need to do is to lure the ghost into our trap. Once it's in, takes a minute to spring. Take these rings and pop one onto each pinky finger. They use haptic feedback to guide you.' Kulekvo mimed reeling in a fish on a line while Doom looked on, baffled. 'Then hook the fishy and into the basket it goes.'

Doom blinked at the two metal rings in her palm as Kulekvo wandered off, chatting enthusiastically to someone on the other end of a call. She turned her attention back to the drinks machine where she'd last seen the woman. Why had the ghost made contact with her at all? Did it know it was her target? This wasn't impossible in theory, yet it would mean that data systems on Satellite Five were as leaky as a colander.

*Target is aware. Target can manifest anyplace. Target cannot be strangled, drowned, poisoned or shot. Target has impressive flirting game.*

She noticed then that the small boy had stepped up and was looking at her, hopefully.

'My Da said to ask you to get him a beer. Machine won't serve me grown-up drinks.'

Doom huffed a dramatic sigh. 'Did he, indeed? Anything else I can get him?'

The boy's brow furrowed. 'No . . . Just the beer.'

She winked and reached out for a reassuring pat to the boy's shoulder, but he took a sudden step back.

'Hey, sorry kiddo, my mistake. Hang on, I'll get your dad his beer.' She paced across to the drinks machine, half expecting him to run off and fetch an angry parent, but when she returned the boy apparently hadn't moved. She smiled, relieved he hadn't summoned 'Da'.

*Collaterals are the worst but collaterals with orphaned children? They're the very worst.*

She nodded at the cup of beer she'd placed on a nearby table. 'You can take it to him yourself.'

Deliberately, she looked away. Kids weren't supposed to drink beer and it wasn't her business if this one wanted a taste, but she preferred to maintain a reasonable doubt.

It was time to learn more about Satellite Five and the year 200,003. She wandered further from the party on the main deck towards a room off the main corridor, comprised of wall-to-wall screens with several displaying news. On one she spotted a report from a world that allegedly faced ASTEROID OBLIVION!

This was pretty much the last news she wanted to watch right now – but Doom stiffened when images of the planet came into view. A landscape of snow, ice, lakes and mountains. The image of one mountain began to expand. It looked sickeningly familiar. She flicked open the control panel in the arm of a nearby sofa and selected audio from that screen.

*'Opposing factions on the planet Vassta squabble over religious beliefs as a stray asteroid threatens to obliterate their civilisation.'*

Doom paled. Vassta? Wasn't that where Stalgon was from? She paused the newscast while she checked details of the previous mission. It was.

*Bad. Very bad. Extremely non-ideal.*

She resumed the broadcast, now fully alert.

*'One faction known as the "Kadhs" are appealing to Vassta's leadership, urging them to destroy the asteroid and save their world. But Abo Chenoute, speaking for the opposing "Mahds" led by an austere order of mystics, issued a statement condemning any interference with the path of Fate and declared, "A blessing upon the Noble and Cleansing Fire that descends from the Realms of Power to destroy all that is evil on Vassta".'*

Doom began to snort in disbelief, then stopped.

*What did I just hear?*

# Cosplay

The newscast began to display a computer model of the asteroid's descent. It began from the vantage point of the rock hurtling through space trailing an icy tail, and then as it entered the planet's atmosphere became engulfed in flames and burned a path all the way to the mountain she recognised. Then it switched to images of the rock in space, which looked like they might be actual photographs.

*'The asteroid, whose origin is as yet unknown, appears to be composed of ice, minerals and an unknown composite material. Scientists on Vassta have theorised that it is an escaped chunk of space waste from an inhabited moon of the gas giant in their planetary system, and are demanding that those responsible commit to paying for the evacuation of their world.'*

Doom paused the newscast again, this time to study the image of the asteroid.

*So that's what you look like. Hideous rock.*

Now Abo Chenoute himself from the Mahd faction was being interviewed. He spoke in the smooth tones of a polished communicator.

*'The wilfulness of the Kadh elites is an attack on the peoples of Vassta. It is a challenge to everyone, a total denial of our being, the overthrow of our faith and traditional values. Moreover, the suppression of liberty itself has taken on the aspect of a religion: outright demon worship. It is to this evil that the Noble and Cleansing Fire from the Realms of Power is addressed. And all Vassta must welcome our fate with humble submission.'*

Doom shook her head in revulsion. How could anyone even pretend to welcome such apocalyptic horror? Meanwhile, this 'Chenoute' fellow probably had his own fast ship off the planet and was using the narrative to grift Mahd cultists until the end.

*Idiots like Chenoute are why the Lesser Order of Oberon* needs *to exist.*

In Stalgon's simulation, however, Vassta had survived; pockmarked and maybe hundreds of thousands dead, but not the planet-busting cataclysm it would have been without the last-minute intervention of the spaceship. Which – she guessed – had been sent by the Kadh faction. When the Kadh spokesman appeared on the newscast insisting that the asteroid be destroyed, Doom's curiosity spiked. She froze the image.

The Kadh's outfit was identical to the uniform worn by the young boy who'd spoken to her.

It made no sense. Unless the boy was from Vassta? Doom's eyes scoured the room until she found the kid. At the opposite end of the lounge, he stood alone beside the broad screen, which now displayed the

Earth on the opposite side of the station. She made a stealthy approach on an intercepting path in case the boy tried to run off. But he didn't budge and barely acknowledged her arrival.

She checked over her shoulder in case 'Da' was close. There was only one other unaccompanied person in the lounge, a human who hadn't moved from her stool the whole time Doom had been on the station. Was this 'Da'? They didn't seem particularly interested in her or the boy, but that didn't mean they weren't keeping a subtly watchful eye.

From a respectable distance, Doom tried to strike up conversation. 'So – did you try the beer? Only joking. You didn't, did you?'

The boy turned slowly to face her. Doom backed off a tad.

'I don't drink beer,' the boy replied. 'It's probably good, though. All the food and drink is real today. My Da said so. To welcome Director Cathica.'

'Oh, Director Cathica, she's a bit brilliant, isn't she?' said Doom, hoping that the ghost-woman's small talk had been historically accurate. 'Talked the Empress into improving the food, she did. So that's good.'

He looked unconvinced. 'My Da says the Fourth Empire should never have been recreated.'

Doom nodded. 'Good point. Love a bit of anarchy, me. So, can I ask, where'd you get the outfit?'

The boy didn't seem to understand the question.

'School uniform, is it? From Vassta?'

Shrugging, the kid said, 'It's just what I wear.'

Increasingly nervous, Doom rotated slowly, looking

for 'Da'. Still nothing. No one seemed to be looking out for the boy. A sense of unease crept over her. Either this kid was being dangerously neglected, or else the lounge was under surveillance and any second now someone might spring out from behind a door to rightly ask what she was doing.

She tried a different tack. 'Did you notice that woman who was talking to me?' Again the boy responded with a blank look. 'Lovely turquoise dress. Brown hair, blue eyes, nice smile, really pretty. A human woman. No?' Doom sighed. It'd been a while since she'd spent real time with her cousins' children. Apparently she'd forgotten how to talk to kids.

But then from the main door emerged the woman herself. *The ghost.* She was alone but sashayed between small groups, smiling and apparently exchanging pleasantries.

*Or is she?*

Doom's eyes narrowed as she concentrated. Were the other people *actually* responding to the woman, or was she reading too much into their smiles and laughs? Perhaps they were just chatting to each other?

'That's her,' Doom said, pointing out the woman on the deck.

'Who?'

'Turquoise dress, from before. Y'know, at the drinks machine?' Doom studied the lad's face. He seemed genuinely bewildered. 'You really can't see her?'

It seemed pretty conclusive – the woman was a ghost. A devious ghost that knew how to blend in, but nevertheless, as ethereal as a hologram.

But in that moment the boy shot Doom a withering

stare. There was something deeply unnerving about it. A horrible thought occurred to her. It made little sense for a young boy to be dressed like the spokesman of a political faction from a distant planet. A ghost, however, might just wear the same outfit – so long as their creator had access to image files of the uniform.

Corinthian resurrection took all extant data about a person and placed it into a simulacrum of their preferred earthly form, usually the person at their peak of adult health and beauty. Most dying people chose an avatar of themselves aged around thirty, which was why she'd assumed the ghost was the woman who'd spoken to her.

There was no technical reason why a ghost couldn't appear as a young boy dressed like a Kadh. Especially if one of the top news stories in the galaxy was the impending destruction of Vassta.

*What if the boy is the ghost? And he can't see Turquoise Dress because he's not haunting her?*

# Floor 500

Doom had to get word to the producer. If the trap Kulekvo had set for the ghost depended on the description she'd supplied, then at best precious minutes were being wasted and at worst the whole enterprise was a bust. She had to find out for sure.

The boy or the woman – which was the ghost? Both had initiated contact. Neither appeared to have seen the other. The woman was the right age, the boy was oddly dressed. That's all she really had to go on.

*The kid ordered horchata. Then asked me for a beer. Ghosts don't drink.*

Then she remembered – she hadn't actually *witnessed* the boy drinking; she'd intentionally looked away before he had a chance to touch the beer. But this logic presented her with a solution. She stormed across the lounge and snatched a freshly poured cup of horchata just as another guest was reaching for it. 'Sorry. Dealing with a bit of a situation.'

With cup in hand, she marched back to the observation deck. 'Hey kiddo, why not have a bit more horchata?'

The boy looked from the drink to Doom and back.

*Great job, Doom. Literally hassling a nine-year old.*

'Or don't. It's up to you.'

She was trying hard to navigate a line between tetchy and approachable. If he really was the ghost then some kind of malevolent genius had dreamed up the avatar. She didn't even want to be *talking* to a make-believe kid let alone killing what looked like one.

Slowly, the boy shook his head. A transformation came over his features, as it had moments before when she'd shot Doom the withering look. There was little trace of a young boy in this expression. He seemed suddenly old and weary.

'Leave me be,' the boy said, with such finality that Doom couldn't respond. 'Don't you have work to do?'

Dazed, she watched the kid wander back across the lounge. When she blinked, he was gone. She went straight to an information port and called Kulekvo. All doubt had vanished.

'I made a mistake. The ghost is a kid, a boy, nine or ten, dressed like the Kadh leader from Vassta. *Why?* Not the foggiest.'

'Not to worry,' came the producer's laidback reply. 'I'm sending the route to your haptic rings. Keep an eye on the arrows.'

Seconds later she sensed a buzzing from in her right

hand. On the ring a faint green arrow was pointing towards the elevator shaft. She set off.

Doom was irked. She *never* accepted jobs that involved assassinating a child – a red line for her and many other hitters of the Lesser Order. A handful saw things differently and invoked the 'ought you kill Hitler as a child?' dilemma. In the previous hour, in self-defence she'd shot what she'd believed to be a child. During the minutes before she'd discovered it was an android, she had felt something she rarely experienced in her work – guilt.

Avoidance of guilt was an important reason for the Lesser Order's knightly code. Otherwise, why bother being part of the Lesser Order of Oberon? Plenty of private gigs if you didn't care about ethics. A ghost wasn't a child. It wasn't even a real human. This one was merely the post-death form of a person who for some bizarro reason had chosen to haunt people by 'resurrecting' their nine-year old form.

*Terri! Would it be too much trouble to do a bit more research? Talk to a client once in a while. 'Hi, can I get just a few more details about the target? Age, gender, maybe a description?'*

This job was messed up, even by the standards of the Lesser Order, who accepted almost any assignment so long as a hitter could be found who'd square it in their personal interpretation of the ethos.

Yet, as she rode the elevator up to Floor 500, she couldn't stop thinking about the way the boy had asked, 'Don't you have work to do?' Not dismissively, not sneering. No – the ghost had seemed *interested,* intrigued. Maybe it didn't believe it could be destroyed?

When the elevator doors opened, the TV producer was waiting. He peered to either side of Doom. 'Is it here?'

'Do your cameras see anything?'

Kulekvo checked his phone. 'No.'

Doom gave a mirthless smile. 'But he'll be here. And soon. So, quickly – what's the plan?'

The producer looked eager. 'I've been dying to show off our set.'

He walked her onto Floor 500. A light smattering of powdery snow covered the floor. The walls were broken in places. A chilly breeze occasionally gusted around them. In the centre of the deck was a circular arrangement of transparent plastic sheeting that hung down from the ceiling. Doom drew aside one of the plastic curtains, stepping back with caution. The whole place was probably boobytrapped. Within was a suite of seats encircling a reclining chair. In every seat lay the mummified remains of a human being, a person who'd died in dreadful rictus.

'Mummies? Bit corny, no?'

'It's a reconstruction.' The producer's eyes were wide and earnest. 'Something terrible happened on Floor 500. A true horror.'

Doom poked the nearest skeleton with her index finger. 'That's quite realistic.'

'Oh, it's absolutely real. I purchased the remains myself.'

Fastidiously, Doom withdrew. She was almost interested enough to ask for the story behind the spooky scenario, but her timer was showing only twenty-seven minutes remaining. 'I'm loving the Halloween sandwich,' she commented. 'But where's the filling?'

'You mean, how do we catch the ghost? That's the tasty part.'

Kulekvo began to walk again, his footsteps crunching in the snow. At the other end of the deck was a second elevator shaft. Doom hadn't noticed anything similar on the other floors.

'The elevator shafts on Satellite Five are lined with panels made from an abzantium composite. Abzantium is 400 times harder and denser than diamond. The panels aren't very thick, but a little goes a long way.'

Doom recalled what 'Professor Yoon' had begun to say about ghosts existing within a certain range of densities. 'And the ghost . . . can't pass through it?'

The producer bristled with pride. 'A Corinthian ghost can pass through normal walls, no problem. But this' – he tapped the dummy elevator door – 'this has been modified. All we need do is to lure your ghost into this elevator, crash it to the bottom of the shaft 500 levels below, drop a carefully positioned extra panel of abzantium composite onto the top and set off a few tiny explosions to fuse the top panel to the rest, forging a secure containment chamber. The ghost will not be able to leave. It'll eke out its remaining existence inside until it runs out of whatever power has been allocated by Corinth Inc. And our viewers can pore over every second of its misery. Let's hope whoever sent it opted for the deluxe power package!'

Doom punched the elevator door button and waited.

The doors opened on a drab interior, four metallic walls and the usual, claustrophobically low ceiling of a space-station elevator. A hellish way to die, for a living being. Would the boy-ghost 'feel' anything?

*Nah. It's just data cosplaying as a person.*

# *Ghost v Assassin*

She wasn't sure when Kulekvo had started filming but it seemed safe to assume Doom had been streamed across the galaxy from the instant she'd set foot on the haunted deck. The producer had pointed out a couple of hidden cameras and boasted that Floor 500 was rigged throughout.

'We miss nothing! Every whisper, every visible emotion recorded. Our viewers can practically *smell* the fear. And they *love* it.'

After some tedious pleasantries, the producer had left Doom alone to roam the frost-bitten 'set'. It was Doom's first time doing reality TV. She had not the remotest interest in how she was received by viewers. Yet it crossed her mind that this might be a way to reach out to the Doctor.

*Like a time traveller's message-in-a-bottle.*

She wandered Floor 500, speaking quietly. 'Doctor, if

you ever happen to see this, I'd love to invite you for a coffee. Cake too, if you fancy. Or pizza, or pasta. Or just soup and a salad. Anything, really. There's something I badly need to ask you about that time we bumped into each other in New Venice. Remember? You, me, the moon, the masks, Saint Mark's looking fully splendid, all lit up in purple and gold. Pesky future-me poking her weapon where it's not wanted. All flooding back now, hopefully? So, *Doctor,* if you remember meeting me at the ball, if you're, y'know, the *same* guy, then it'd be brilliant to hear from you. Sooner the better, ideally. I'm on Floor 500 of Satellite Five in the year 200,003. You can get the exact date from the show. Lots of love.'

Doom returned her attention to the surroundings. The mummified remains were obviously a highlight but, as she explored further, the haunted-house theme continued. In broken chairs before a row of monitors now dead, cracked and dusted with snow, sat more human remains; frozen in place, their empty eye sockets staring at forever-blank screens. She wondered what 'terrible' something had happened on the ill-fated Floor 500 of which this was a reconstruction, and how long ago. Had these people been worked to death at their stations, or died mercifully quick deaths?

Her foot knocked against something rock hard. When she shone a light onto it she recoiled in horror. She'd bumped into what looked like part of an animal's lower jaw. A giant shark, perhaps. Or an alien. The bone fragment contained at least a dozen long, triangular teeth, several layers deep and up to thirty centimetres long. She flashed her light around the area, eyes now attuned and hunting for anything else similar. A few minutes later she located another chunk. It was too macabre to touch with her hands so she used both feet to shuffle it closer to the first piece. She was in the process of trying – without actually laying a finger on the bones – to reconstruct the creature's lower jaw, when she heard a familiar voice and startled.

'That is disgusting,' the ghost-boy observed.

'Kid, you almost gave me a heart attack!'

The ghost looked at her, detached. 'It's a monster.'

'What gave it away, the masses of spiky teeth? I'm guessing it lived here, once. Made prisoners of these poor goners, probably. Otherwise, I imagine they'd have run off.'

The ghost-boy stood behind her now, so close that a real person would have cast a shadow. Doom straightened up and backed away from the grisly mouth of what must have been a fearsome beast.

'It was known as the Mighty Jagrafess of the Holy Hadrojassic Maxarodenfoe,' the boy said. 'It enslaved the human race. Until three years ago, when Cathica Santini Khadeni led the uprising. She's the Director of Satellite Five now, but back then she was a slave, too.'

'Well, aren't you just a walking history book?' Doom said, stepping back for her first proper look at the ghost. Was this part of the ghost's real memory, or did Corinth Inc. bundle an encyclopaedia into their product?

The boy had gone back to staring into Doom's eyes. After a few seconds it became unnerving.

*Fine, I didn't want to get to know you anyway. Let's get this over with.*

Without checking to see if the ghost followed, she turned and headed for the dummy elevator where Kulekvo's team had laid the ghost-trap. Reaching the elevator shaft, she was relieved to see that the ghost had followed, although at a distance that suggested she mightn't automatically get into the elevator.

'Where are you going?' asked the ghost-boy.

There it was again – the oddly adult tone. He sounded faintly amused, as if he knew there was something fishy about the whole set-up but had decided to play along. Or was Doom simply projecting her own fears about this ghost?

She stabbed the elevator button with her index finger and tried to look insouciant. 'Off this floor, that's for sure. It's rubbish here. Nothing to eat or drink.'

'Then why did you come?'

'Well, something to do, isn't it? Haunted houses . . . they're always worth a visit.'

The elevator doors opened. Doom manoeuvred aside, inviting the ghost to enter first. But the boy just continued to stare. An awkward silence lengthened to the point of embarrassment.

'Shouldn't you be getting back to your dad?'

The boy gave a single, solemn nod.

Doom tipped her head towards the interior. 'In you pop, then.'

The boy stepped inside, eyes not leaving Doom's. His gaze became expectant. 'Aren't you going to take me to my Da?'

Doom sighed. 'Fine.'

The boy held the elevator doors open. She stepped

inside, ready to sneak out at the last second just before the doors closed. But the instant she was inside the doors snapped shut with such violence that Doom was pretty sure she'd have been sliced in half if she'd tried to escape.

The elevator didn't move, at first. She tried to smile at the boy and failed. Seconds ticked past, twenty, forty, a minute. Then her cover broke. She began to bang on the doors, yelling, 'Hey. Big problem, here. Open up.'

The elevator began to fall. Over a hidden loudspeaker the voice of the producer gleefully intoned, 'Now the hunter has become the hunted and both specimens will face the end together!'

All sense of decorum vanished, like smoke. Doom hurled her fist over and over against the elevator doors, screaming as the box that would shortly become her tomb dropped down the elevator shaft. 'Stop this thing, let me out!'

'My dear,' cackled Kulekvo, 'why on *earth* would I do a silly thing like that? *Ghost v Assassin* could only ever end this way. Billions of viewers will watch, rapt at the spectacle of you being blown apart and then the ghost fizzling out weeks later after watching your corpse slowly fester!'

# FALLING

'Listen to me. It's very important that you listen. You need to get out of here, right now. Flow through the ceiling or whatever it is you ghosts do. Find a gap in the walls of the shaft, get as far from it as you can.'

The ghost-boy just stared. *Why did it have to look like a child? It's not a child!*

In frustration she cried out loud, 'Why even offer me this job, Terri? There are *heaps* of assassins that'll kill literally anything!' She glared at the ghost. 'Get out, understand? Right now.' She pointed up. 'Through the ceiling. The walls are lined with abzantium. It's too dense for your molecular structure. Find a hatch, a gap, anything.'

Still the ghost seemed to be paralysed, so she screamed in its face. 'Kid, just GO!'

Petrified, she watched the floor numbers whoosh past: *350 . . . 340 . . . 330 . . .*

For another desperate second, Doom wondered if whatever powered the ghost had frozen, because the boy didn't budge. But then, with a speed she hadn't anticipated, he appeared to levitate, disappearing through the ceiling.

There wasn't time to breathe a sigh of relief. She selected another job at random and prepared to punch out of the job early. It was a last gasp with almost no chance of working, but for once Terri's incompetence might save Doom. If a Lesser Order account manager failed properly to check the kill against all relevant timelines, the chances were slim that a request would be accepted.

*220 . . . 210 . . . 200 . . .*

She stared at the vortex manipulator's display screen, barely able to hope for a positive response.

*EARLY COMPLETION REQUEST REJECTED.*

Doom dropped to her knees, moaning in despair and clutching her face in both hands. She half-expected the cowled figure to visit her one last time.

*Better not to look.*

The message she'd left for the Doctor was now the only possible 'Hail Mary'. The sensation of pressure inside her ribcage became almost overwhelming, the sheer terror of being trapped, literally entombed.

From above her head she heard a brisk whistle. A hatch had opened in the low ceiling. The ghost-boy's head popped into view. He beckoned Doom with a finger. She leapt to her feet and, with every scrap of energy and hope and desperation in her body, launched herself at the hatch with both arms outstretched. There wasn't time for a second attempt and she knew it.

With her right hand she managed to catch hold of the edge. She followed through with her left, then groaning with effort she dragged herself through the hatch.

*Second time today. If I live, I'm adding full-body pull-ups to my workout.*

The ghost-boy was waiting on top of the descending elevator, crouching. It was plummeting too fast for anything but a random jump with both hands flailing, grabbing whatever they could reach on the sides of the shaft.

Doom didn't hesitate. She closed her eyes and leapt. Her entire body slapped against a smooth, flat wall. Immediately, she slid down. Her palms began to burn from the friction as she accelerated. Her ears roared with the sound of the elevator falling further away until suddenly, it stopped. Then from above came a sound that made her heartrate quicken so fast she felt her head might explode from the burst of pressure. High at the top of the shaft something had detached and was dropping, dimming what little light there was in the shaft as it tumbled.

She heard the ghost-boy shouting, 'Reach right, right, right!'

There wasn't time to think – she threw out her right arm, fingers reaching for anything at all. Her knuckles cracked as they encountered a protruding bar of metal. She held on tight and swung herself over. It was a doorhandle. Darkness loomed as the shadow of the final piece of the death-trap approached to complete their intended coffin. Doom pushed down on the handle and leaned hard against the door. If it didn't open inwards, she was finished.

She crashed into a corridor, falling heavily onto her right side. For several seconds, she could only catch her breath. Gradually she opened her eyes, groaning at the throbbing in her shoulder. Standing over her was the ghost-boy. The blank stare was gone. Now the kid looked utterly amazed.

'You *let* me go.'

Doom struggled to her feet. 'I'd have died before you did so . . . Y'know. Might as well.'

'Did you know there was an escape hatch?'

'Well, did *you* see one?'

The boy shook her head. 'Not from the inside, no. Then you really and truly freed me.'

'Kiddo, this isn't personal. If I'm not around to pick up the fee for your demise, why wouldn't I save you? By the way, how d'you open it?'

'I can focus the energy of my molecular matrix to press buttons, carry light objects.'

'Got it, like horchata and beer. Isn't that nice. Right, then.' Doom dusted herself off. Her shoulder hurt like crazy, was probably dislocated. 'Thanks for the rescue. Lovely as it'd be to chit-chat and all, I need to find some first aid. Then I'm going to deal with our friend, Mr Producer.'

'I see,' the ghost-boy said. 'And after that? What's your next job?'

'Haven't picked one yet. Thank goodness, because I could use a break.'

'Billions of viewers just watched you escape a death-trap,' the ghost reminded her. 'Are you safe on Satellite Five?'

Doom let out a ragged sigh. 'Doubt it. Hence the freebie on the producer. That blowhard is going to be sorry he ever tangled with someone from the Lesser Order.'

'Then you would kill for a grudge, as well as for money?'

Irritated, Doom nevertheless made an effort to maintain a light tone. 'Not just a historian, I see. Now you're a professor of ethics, too?'

The ghost smiled, slyly. 'If you're going to assassinate the producer, can I come, too?'

# TRUTHING

'How do you pick a mission? And what kind of people hire you? How will you kill the producer? Why did he want us dead, do you know?'

Doom already regretted agreeing to the tag-along. The ghost-boy trotted beside her, apparently struggling to keep up with adult-length strides as she thundered towards the main elevator shaft on Floor 85. For the first time since they'd met, the ghost was behaving like an actual nine-year-old: it couldn't stop asking questions.

Through gritted teeth she replied, 'I look at the fee. People with money and a grudge. Usually I'd finesse it more but time's an issue so I thought I'd just shoot the jerk. Since you mention it, yeah, it'd be good to know if he had any specific reason – other than for the lols. I dunno, maybe I'll truth him to death.'

'What's "truth him to death"?'

At an information terminal, Doom came to a stop.

Her right shoulder ached and she could barely raise her right arm. Her palms had friction burns and two fingers on her right hand were broken, something she'd only noticed a few seconds ago. As the shock and adrenalin subsided, her brain seemed to be reconnecting with her body, like a robot performing a systems check. All was definitely not well.

She placed her hand on the palm-shaped depression in the terminal and called Kulekvo. He didn't pick up. Then she said aloud, 'Where is the TV studio?'

The pleasant voice replied, 'There are nine television production companies on Satellite Five.'

'Which one produces . . . ? Dammit, what was the name of the show?'

'*Ghost v Whatever,*' chimed the ghost.

'*Ghost v Whatever.*'

'The reality show *Ghost v Whatever* is a production of the Telluric TV Company located on Floor 267, office suite 16.'

Doom clicked her fingers and set off. 'Let's go.'

Following close behind, the boy repeated. 'What's "truthing to death"?'

They arrived seconds too late to catch the elevator. Doom summoned another then leaned against the wall on her left side nursing two broken fingers while she waited.

'I give him an overdose of a drug that makes it exceedingly difficult to lie. If I get the dose right, before he dies he spills the beans.'

'Does it hurt?'

'You're a ghost. What do you care?'

'I'm interested in your work. I believe you are good at it?'

'You'd be pushed to find anyone better,' Doom said, without a drop of false modesty. 'Sort of fell into it after the music career didn't pan out and I ran into a spot of bother with . . . Oh, it doesn't matter. Anyway, didn't think I'd do this for long but . . . yeah. It stuck. Like a summer job you never get around to leaving.'

Her competence had come as a surprise. It was addictive to find yourself so good at something, although it'd gotten more difficult since the incident on New Venice. Today she'd several times been horribly close to death and, despite narrow escapes, with every passing second she sensed the inexorable approach of death.

*Today is not clever and it's not funny.*

'What does it feel like to be "truthed to death"?'

'I've had folk look me right in the eyes and tell me it feels amazing, if you must know,' Doom said, loftily.

'Your victims?'

'They weren't complaining,' she snapped.

The elevator had arrived. She entered and chose Floor 267 without bothering to wait for the ghost.

But the kid apparated through the closed doors as the elevator set off upwards. He turned to her. 'Say more.'

'You feel giddy. Then light. Then the cares of the world drift away, lift off into space. There's a sense of immense wellbeing. You know you're going to die and you're not bothered. There's an urge to right all the wrongs in your life, to confess. Most people talk *all the way* to unconsciousness. They babble incessantly. If you ask the right questions they're only too happy to tell you anything. And it's always true because—'

'Because they want to confess?'

'Right. They know they're in the final moments of life, when almost everyone wants to be seen, *really* seen. To feel empathy. And they tell the truth.'

'Then they die?'

'They go out like a light. So you see, I'm doing Kulekvo a favour. More than he did for you or me. That sadist was going to turn our suffering into entertainment.'

'How is that a favour?' The ghost reflected. 'You'd have died instantly and I can't suffer.'

Doom sniped, 'I don't believe we had an ethics tutorial scheduled for today, Professor Ghost.'

'Oh. You're angry.'

She fell silent, seething. But the ghost had a point. Doom didn't want to kill Kulekvo, however smarmy the producer was, however badly she'd been tricked. But she did need to know she'd be safe on Satellite Five – at least long enough to heal her shoulder and fingers and to treat her friction burns. These past two missions had felt like being thrown into an arena with gladiators.

*I'm not going into another until I'm fixed. Hopefully a cosy poisoning in the bar of a luxury hotel next time.*

Even before they arrived at the offices of the Telluric TV Company, Doom sensed something awry. The main door was open and uniformed security guards were milling about outside. Their sidearms remained holstered but clearly visible. One of them caught her eye from a few metres away. The guard looked instantly suspicious and drew a weapon.

Doom pivoted and began to walk briskly in the opposite direction. Two seconds later the guard called out, 'Hey, you! Stop!'

She broke into a run, heading for the emergency stairs. She leapt the steps two at a time, didn't stop until she heard the door open three floors above. She bolted out of the staircase and made a dash for the elevator. For once she was in luck, it arrived within a few seconds. Inside she requested Floor 500 and held the door open, drew her staser pistol and tucked it out of sight under her left arm.

The security guard arrived a moment later, panting for breath. Seeing Doom inside and the doors still open, a satisfied grin spread across the guard's face. She drew a chunky handgun. 'Get out. You're wanted for questioning about the death of Andre Kulekvo.'

Doom frowned. *The producer is already a goner?* Then she released the door button. 'Make me.'

# Alexyi

The guard stepped into the lift. As the doors began to close behind her, a wily grin flickered at the edges of her mouth. 'Not so clever now, are we? Floor 325.'

Doom spotted the ghost slip into the elevator behind the security guard. Backing away, she watched the ethereal raise its finger to the control panel. Just as the doors were about to snap shut, the kid pressed the 'doors open' button.

Doom jumped backwards through the widening gap a fraction of a second before the ghost switched to the 'closed' button. Instinctively, she flung herself face-first to the ground. From inside the elevator, the security guard fired, all three shots whizzing over Doom's head, roughly where her chest had been. Then the elevator was gone. A moment later the ghost walked out through the closed doors.

'Nice save,' Doom commented, clambering to her feet.

The ghost-boy didn't seem remotely interested in a discussion but asked bluntly, 'What happens to you if you don't kill me?'

'Nothing particularly good. If I don't, y'know, actually kill my target, well, little by little I'd get a reputation for being generally useless. And I don't get paid, which means no commission for my handlers, which means I might not be able to get another contract quickly, which means I can't easily move on.'

'And that's bad?'

She thought for a second, then decided to share a bit more. 'It means something unpleasant might catch up to me.' She looked around for a floor number, then checked the vortex manipulator's timer. 'Kiddo, I have about fifteen minutes before this hour is up. Then I'm off to the next job, fingers crossed. Meantime, I could use some medical attention. So, I think this is where we say bye-bye.'

She flashed the ghost a brisk smile and set off towards the stairs. The last thing she wanted was to end up being trapped in another elevator.

From behind she heard the boy calling to her. 'I can control my own power, you know. If I power down, could you say you killed me?'

'Depends,' Doom said. 'Are you planning to power up again?'

The ghost sounded puzzled. 'Not if I power down. I need power to do *anything*.'

Doom had reached the emergency stairwell. She stalled, hand on the door. 'Who switched you on, then?'

'The ship. I'm part of its safety protocol. A millisecond

before the ship was destroyed all its data was transferred to the server on Corinth. My avatar was created and sent here.'

'*What* ship? Oh, hang on . . . seriously? *No*. The asteroid-smasher? That was *you*?'

'In a way. I'm the ship's *memory*. I had to find you. See, I know a place you can hide,' the boy added. 'Not here, there are security cameras.' He turned to leave then turned back with solemn eyes. 'Follow me.'

Realisation crept across Doom's shoulders; she felt her cheeks flush as the sensation swept upwards. Now following the ghost down the stairs, her pulse began to race. 'Your clothes,' she said, urgently. It was all starting to make sense. 'You're dressed like the Kadh leader, on Vassta. Why?'

'He's my dad.'

'Your dad? I thought you were a spaceship's memory.'

'I am, but I have to look like an actual person.'

'You're *alive*? I mean, the real version of your avatar?'

'I don't know,' the boy replied, almost cheerful. 'My dad hopes so. This is what I looked like last time he saw me.'

'Which was when?'

'Two years ago.'

'Where does your dad think you are? Again – *real* you.'

The ghost-boy stopped at Floor 79 and passed through the exit to the corridor beyond. Doom opened the door and followed.

'With my mother. They disagreed about the future.'

Doom groaned. 'Oh, mate. She's a Mahd?'

'She is. My dad chose this avatar. I don't know why.'

Doom could guess. It was almost impossible not to feel sympathy for this apparently guileless kid. 'You said you had to find me. Why?'

'Because I heard you. In Stalgon's simulation.'

'Oh, you know about that, too?'

'I was capturing all transmission data in the vicinity until the end. Stalgon was monitoring the entire sim environment while communicating with the Kraals. I heard you say it.'

'Heard me say *what*?'

The boy turned and, to Doom's astonishment and considerable revulsion, she heard her own voice emerge from the kid's mouth.

*'I'd kill that asteroid for free if someone asked; that's how much I hate it.'*

The ghost stopped in front of a door, then opened it. Inside was a storage room lined with shelves stacked with medical supplies. 'I accessed a plan of the station, earlier. This room is in a camera blind spot. You can fix yourself here.'

Doom went inside, closing the door behind her. There was barely space to take more than two paces forward or back. 'Yeah. No. Nice idea, kiddo, but I'm no field medic.'

'The producer is dead,' the boy reminded her bluntly.

'Yeah, about that. How?'

The ghost ignored the question. 'You're the main suspect, you will be arrested again. You should go. I'll power down. You can claim the kill and leave. But first I need to ask you for something.'

Crouching on her haunches, Doom struggled to handle these revelations.

'You said you'd kill the asteroid for free,' the ghost said. 'I want you to do that.'

'Yeaaa . . . People say all sorts, under stress. With me you get no conscience. No mercy. And no discounts.'

'A discount isn't free.'

A helpless laugh escaped her. 'Of course. Of *course* I'd be hired by a ghost. I'm being stalked by Death, why not get hired by a ghost?'

The ghost-boy lowered himself until they were looking each other directly in the eye. And there it was again, the hopeful, trusting face of an innocent child. Doom trembled, uselessly resisting the impulse to protect the lad.

'Not by a ghost. By my *dad,* D'Mitre Tannelo Kadh. He wants to see me grow up. To see all children of Vassta grow up, to have a whole planet, to escape the delusion of the Mahds. Vassta should be cared for, protected, not be destroyed by an asteroid.'

'But the spaceship . . .'

The boy shook his head firmly. 'The spaceship can't stop the destruction. It can only limit the damage. The Mahds have managed to prevent anyone taking action in time. Now it's too late. They paid Stalgon and the Kraals to build the simulation to prove that the asteroid wouldn't destroy the planet, just wreak havoc.'

'And the Mahds think the havoc is "Fate",' recalled Doom.

'Yes. They worship the havoc, they welcome it.'

Both fell silent. Doom closed her eyes, sighing. 'I can't vortex out, not in this condition. I need to be mission-fit.'

'Will you kill the asteroid for me, for the *real* me?'

'Kill an asteroid? Kid, you're hilarious. Even if I could, you'd need to go through the right channels.' She tapped the vortex manipulator. 'Terri has to enter all the details, the precise temporal-spatial coordinates. And I think we've already covered my position on discounts.'

Slowly, the ghost blinked twice. 'Done. Mission PB3005. I selected the "pro bono" request. Oh, look, admin level can pre-set a mission to "success", so the fee gets paid either way.'

'Huh! Wondered what the "PB" meant! Makes sense. I never pick those – the pay automatically goes to charity. Bit noble. Not really me.' Doom stood up. 'All right, then.' She needed to keep the job offers flowing, or become easy prey for her deathly stalker. 'You do the pre-agreed success thing and I'll do it.'

The boy didn't reply, but continued to look hopeful as they watched the start of the countdown to her next mission.

'There's just enough time to pop my shoulder back and get a shot of painkillers and tissue-repair nanites. Off you go, then. Wait, hang on.' She hesitated. 'What's your name? The real you, not your "Da".'

A smile of pure joy spread across the little boy's face. 'I'm Alexyi. Alexyi Tannelo Kadh.' He opened his fist. Inside was her lost monocle tracker. 'Sorry that I took it. I needed you to see me. *Alexyi*. Not just a target.'

# Twelve Hours

# SNAKES

Doom materialised in total darkness. This job called for a spacesuit with helmet, breathing apparatus and radiation-shielding technology that her holosuit couldn't provide. The kit had been vortexed to her coordinates just before she'd left Satellite Five and she now wore the thin radiation suit and air supply under her cloak. The visor of the helmet was pressed against a roughly hewn tunnel wall and her monocle lay in place over the usual eye.

*Huh, cave art. Didn't expect that.*

The wall was covered with paintings. Snakes, painted in ochre, cobalt blue and carmine red, descending diagonally from the top-right corner of the cave, each serpent's coils undulating, their feathered heads paused at a variety of distances from the floor.

Stepping back, she made a few basic safety checks: monocle tracker, oxygen supply, suit thermals. All functioning normally. She waited while the tracker ran a l light detection scan of the asteroid then produced a map of its tunnels. There was enough air to complete the hour, although Doom was confident she'd be leaving this job early. She'd plant fission spikes over the next twenty minutes, set a timer and then vortex out before the explosion. There was a chance she'd still fail to divert the asteroid and forfeit the payday, but that was the risk she'd take.

Apparently, vortexing out before a confirmed kill *was* an option on pro-bono jobs. The whole pro-bono world was new to her and, Doom couldn't help thinking, sniffed distinctly suss. If you weren't killing for money, then what? Pleasure? Revenge?

'I'll give it one go, Alexyi, for you and your "Da". But don't expect me to stick around to confirm. Not having my atoms scattered all over Vassta, not for anyone.'

They'd been her last words to the ghost before it had powered down. The 'completion' fee for Ghost-Alexyi's demise had been transferred seconds later, which meant that automatic death-verifications had been enough. Terri herself was never so prompt. Minutes later, Doom had checked into a private clinic on Satellite Five, bribed the technician to ignore the fact he was treating the most wanted person on board and walked out with thirty-two seconds remaining on the timer, shoulder restored and freshly synthesised skin coating her burns. Together with a cocktail of 'wellbeing' neurotransmitters and hormones coursing through her veins, she'd rarely felt better.

The sight of cave art inside the asteroid, therefore, was unexpected and jarring.

*Am I in the right place?*

The vortex manipulator seemed to be working fine – it read fifty-eight minutes remaining on the hour. Her dispatch app showed Mission PB3005 currently active: 'Destroy asteroid before it crashes into Vassta. Client – Alexyi Tannelo Kadh of Vassta.'

Doom noticed something that she was fairly certain hadn't been there when she took the job. The mission brief had a message attached. It appeared to have come from the client, but that had to be wrong because she'd watched the ghost fizzle out at least half an hour before she accepted the job. Then again, this client wasn't your run-of-the-mill, sentient organic being type of client, but rather a sentient form of data.

She clicked on the message. It was a video, a newscast with the same branding she'd seen on the public decks of Satellite Five. Alexyi had told her 'he' had harvested the spaceship's data until the millisecond before it was destroyed. Could the ship's memory-avatar have done the same thing with Satellite Five's data?

Doom played the video.

*Residents of Satellite Five are urged to be on the lookout for a newly minted reality TV star, the human female assassin and karaoke artiste known as 'Doom'. Security forces need to question Miz Doom about the gruesome murder of Andre Kulekvo, producer of the smash hit TV show* Ghost v Whatever, *whose body was rumoured to be found mutilated in a bizarre fashion although reporters have been unable to find any witness to provide reliable details. All we know so far is that only one organ of the body has been located, while the search for the rest is ongoing. As well as being wanted by security forces, the assassin, whom billions of viewers watched escape a potentially tragic accident during the filming of the episode titled* Ghost v Assassin, *is sought by three major broadcasters offering a substantial fee for an interview and the rights to Miz Doom's life story. Anyone bringing information leading to either her arrest or her interview can be sure of a handsome reward. Although one suspects it's rather more handsome in the case of the latter.*

In mounting bewilderment, Doom watched the video two more times. Kulekvo's death must have happened at around the same time as his own scheme to murder her and trap the ghost, because the first attempt to arrest her had taken place mere minutes afterward. It was hard to believe she was even a suspect; surely she'd barely been unaccounted for long enough to fit in another 'hit' with a side of 'mutilation' while making her own escape.

'If all they found was one organ, it's probably because he got too close to his own boobytrap,' Doom muttered to herself. She peered more closely at the snake paintings. They appeared crudely drawn, like cave art of early human civilisations. Those folk usually painted bison and mastodons, noble creatures of the hunt, didn't they? Snakes struck her as out of place and weirdly unnerving. Like some kind of warning.

*Cave art . . . Asteroid? Nope.*

From the shadows behind her, Doom heard a rustle. Snakes on her mind, she swung round, casting the beam of her headlamp onto the rough ground. The rustling – definitely not the swishy type you might associate with slithering animals – became more frenzied as she tracked it with the light. Beneath a thin layer of thermally controlled fabric her skin prickled as the hairs on her neck and arms stood on end. Slowly, reluctantly, she shifted the light towards the far end of the tunnel, more than five metres away. A dark mass seemed to be accumulating there, piling higher as the beam of light approached. Doom's mind took another second to process what she was seeing. Then she froze, shuddering in revulsion.

A two-metre-tall column of cinnamon-brown *somethings* was teetering as the units at the top began to unbalance the whole. As a few began to fall away, they hit the ground and shimmered a neon orange for a second before scuttling away from the light. Casting the light this way and that, increasingly panicked, Doom watched as they headed in every direction aiming for whatever shade they could get. And she could still hear them: thousands of tiny feet scraping and scratching through the fine dust layering the ground. Finally, for just a second she caught one in the full beam of her headlamp. It was a cockroach, huge, at least twenty centimetres long. Bristling with rage and aggression and along with hundreds of others, headed straight for Doom.

# Insects

They began to fall on her from the roof of the tunnel. The first one to land shimmered briefly, a flare of neon orange on her left shoulder before she knocked it away with the back of her hand. The next landed on her outstretched arm – she flung it away before it even had a chance to light up. But then they descended by the half-dozen, gripping the fabric of her thermal suit with their myriad tiny claws and activating whatever drove their phosphorescence. Within a minute she was surrounded by enough glowing orange light to see exactly the fate that would imminently befall her. Hundreds of giant cockroaches bore down on her, swarming from the recesses of the cavern. She could feel them stabbing at the suit, attempting to penetrate through to her flesh.

Doom staggered as they heaped onto her, the weight of them threatening to topple her. She was so appalled she couldn't even breathe, let alone scream. They were all over her helmet now, scurrying and turning as if to locate any chink in the suit. From behind the visor she saw the underbelly of one particularly large specimen, watched its six articulated legs wriggling in that oddly robotic manner of insects. Another ancient species memory within her brain seemed to activate, an overwhelming sense of disgust followed by a vicious rage. She began to beat at the bugs with both hands, knocking them off her helmet, smashing as many as she could underfoot. Her entire body seemed to be consumed with violence. Each fresh crunch beneath her feet filled her with pure satisfaction. Oxygen rushed into her lungs as she remembered to breathe.

'Die, disgusting insects! Aaarghhh!'

Still they kept coming. No sooner had she cleared most away than more followed, leaping onto her from the walls and roof of the tunnel, filling the space with their pulsating neon light. The column of cockroaches was almost half its original size now, and she was already tired. Doom began to realise that she was almost spent. The tsunami of murderous violence towards the insects dissipated. Nothing remained but fear. She knocked one more cockroach from the visor and turned. Just then, she felt a sharp prick to her right shoulder as one of the insects managed to pierce the fabric.

Something grabbed her left hand and tugged.

'Run.'

Dragged by whoever – or whatever – had her hand firmly in their grip, Doom sprinted for at least a hundred metres without stopping. Somewhere along the line, whoever was pulling her along released her hand but she kept running, spurred on by the incessant sound of insectoid scuttling. When she finally slowed down, she had the presence of mind to check her oxygen levels. The suit had been calibrated for seventy minutes at medium effort – a reasonable balance between weight and what was the usual level of physical expenditure during an assignment. Now only fifty-two minutes of air remained.

*Plenty of time to lay charges, then I'm out. No more disgusting bugs.*

Doom was still bent over catching her wind, when a cheery voice reached her.

'There you are! Don't hang about, do you? I like that. Tell some folk to run and they just stare at you all gormless, but you? One word and you're doing the ten-second dash.'

From the shadows emerged the tall, blue-eyed and leather-coated figure of the Doctor she'd seen seconds before she'd vortexed out of the Kraal simulation of Vassta's final hour.

'Good to see you again, Doom. By the way, you don't need a spacesuit here. There's oxygen, weirdly enough. TARDIS is still working out where it's coming from.'

The Doctor grinned widely, pointing a finger at his helmet-free face. Doom hesitated for another second, depressurised the suit and slowly removed the helmet. Taking a few experimental breaths, she sniffed the air. It tasted fresh, no hint of staleness.

Once again resting hands on her thighs, Doom began to laugh with relief. 'My gosh. It really is you. Of course, why wouldn't it be? Sheesh. What a day. If I told you, you'd never believe it.'

'Try me,' grinned the Doctor, close enough for Doom to notice the blue twinkle of his eyes. 'So, who've you been sent to see off this time? Not me, I hope?' The Doctor chuckled, but Doom thought she heard something forced.

'This,' Doom replied, making a vague, expansive gesture. 'The whole shebang.'

'I got your message,' the Doctor said, lightly. 'One benefit of being a Time Lord – doesn't matter if a message takes a while to find its way to the TARDIS. Imagine my surprise when I saw little ol' you muttering under your breath about *me* on a live TV show.'

'How'd you know I was here?'

The Doctor placed a friendly arm round her shoulders. 'Had a word with Terri, at your work.'

Shocked, Doom blurted, 'Doctor, that is *well* out of line!'

He gave a merry chortle. 'Nah, you're all right, I'm just kidding. I guessed you'd come here, once you found out about the Kraal simulation. You and this rock, you've obviously got unfinished business.' His beaming grin returned. 'I thought I'd help you out.'

'Ohhh, I get it. Feeling guilty about not helping me with my other problem, are we?'

The grin vanished. 'No need to get shirty. Don't you want a hand, then?'

She tapped her rucksack. 'All good, thanks. I've got fission spikes. Make asteroid go boom.'

The Doctor considered this. 'Yeah, might do the trick. Better than the spaceship, anyway. Turns out almost a million people still die in that scenario.'

'That won't happen,' declared a new voice. From the shadows behind the Doctor, a woman stepped forward. Doom saw at once that she was a Vasstan with the same dark-honey-coloured eyes, brown skin and similar black-ink facial tattoos to Mandra's, although this woman was older and less athletic. Like the Doctor, she wore no spacesuit, just trousers under a long coat – made of the same light, thermal material as the ski jackets in Svoda – and sturdy boots. She and the Doctor obviously knew something about this place that Doom didn't.

The Vasstan woman approached, holding up both hands so they could see she wasn't armed. 'No one on Vassta is going to die. The simulation you witnessed was flawed.'

'She with you?' Doom asked the Doctor.

'Doom, meet Kat. From Vassta.'

Kat fixed Doom with a calm, confident gaze. 'Destroy this asteroid and you'll practically be committing genocide. The senseless killing of one of the universe's most rare, beautiful and benign life forms. And this one,' she said, with a nod at the Doctor, 'tends to get a bee in his bonnet about things like that.'

# KAT

'Oho, nice try,' the Doctor said to Kat. 'But I don't think so.' He tipped a nod at Doom. 'Doom, as you were.'

Kat didn't miss a beat. 'Doctor, you disappoint me.'

'I'm sorry, did I miss something?' The Doctor's tone had shifted; now Doom detected a steely undertone. 'I thought we were investigating whoever is behind this asteroid attack. How come you're only now telling me about the insects?'

Doom watched in fascination as the layer of charm peeled away and this cheery, casual 'Doctor' seemed to channel someone more familiar – the Time Lord from New Venice.

'We are investigating,' conceded Kat. 'I may have withheld some details.'

Doom guessed that Kat had mis-stepped and was now trying to roll it back.

The Doctor took a step closer to the Vasstan woman.

He scrutinised her closely. 'I don't much like it when people I'm helping keep things from me.'

Slowly, Kat drew a sidearm.

The Doctor didn't flinch. Instead, his gaze seemed to intensify. There was a strained pause. 'Quite sure you want to do that, are you?' he said, eventually.

Kat became belligerent. 'What choice did I have? You took the data from Stalgon's simulation. Without that we cannot evaluate the threat to my world.'

Raising an eyebrow, the Doctor turned to Doom. 'Sure *she* isn't your target? I'm getting a vibe.'

The monocle tracker had Kat marked as a random humanoid – definitely not a target but possibly a threat. Doom's hand was already hovering close to her weapon, ready to draw it in self-defence. This unexpected stranger's appearance was troubling. Was it possible that 'Kat' was telling the truth? Genocide was another of her red lines, never to be crossed. It'd happened once, entirely by accident. Or, at least, it hadn't been her intention. She'd been deceived into eradicating an entire species of butterfly in order to make it easier to terraform a planet. The awareness of what she'd done still preyed on her. It was why she was reluctant to accept jobs where the client was any kind of government leader.

'Why don't you put down the gun and explain what you mean?' Doom said, using her best de-escalatory tone. Anyone who pointed a live weapon at someone in such a confined space was potentially dangerous. Kat, for all her smooth confidence, could end them both in seconds, if she was fast.

'What, and let you draw your own?' Kat replied,

side-eyeing the bulge in Doom's jacket. She stepped out of range of the Doctor's hands and now aimed her weapon at Doom.

Very carefully, Doom moved her hand away from her gun, spreading the fingers so Kat could see they were empty. 'Look, I'm just trying to earn a crust. Not an ideological bone in my body.'

'Who hired you to destroy the asteroid?' Kat barked.

'My gosh,' Doom replied, feigning bashfulness. 'I don't like to say. Client confidentiality and all that.'

'Don't waste your breath,' Kat sneered. 'It hardly matters. I can guess easily enough: the Kadhs. They'd do anything to maintain control over Vassta. Fearmongering, driving hatred of the downtrodden Mahds. They'd even massacre a life form that has absolutely zero intention of harming their world. Why not, if they can blame it on Abo Chenoute and the Mahds?'

Doom tried to discern the Doctor's expression but the Time Lord had now faced away, taking Kat head-on.

'Kat, why are you doing this?' he asked softly.

'I'm sorry I had to lie to you, Doctor. But *we* need Stalgon's data. You had no business taking it. This asteroid is a nest,' she declared emphatically. 'Its entire structure was created in the Kamiclar Belt of this system's largest gas giant. There was an ancient moon there once, inhabited by a species of sentient insectoids. We've found ruins of temples. They had intelligence, they had a society. All of that was obliterated in a collision with another satellite.'

The Doctor seemed to be listening intently. Could it possibly be true?

'I saw some insects,' Doom admitted. 'Didn't seem particularly civilised.'

'Of course not,' said Kat. 'That all happened almost a million of years ago. They've evolved. These insects have a biochemistry that manufactures enough oxygen to thrive. Hence the breathable atmosphere. Moreover, they're able to respond to growing demand – the three of us.'

'And you're – what,' the Doctor asked, sounding ever-so-slightly sceptical. 'An entomologist?'

'As it happens, yes,' snapped Kat. 'I'm the chief astrobiologist of Vassta Space Exploration *and* chair of entomology at the university. We've been studying the Kamiclar Belt ruins for a decade. If either of you actually cared anything about Vassta you'd already know.'

'If you say so,' the Doctor said softly. Very, *very* gradually, he was edging closer to Kat.

Doom exhaled through pursed lips. Why would they know about Vassta? It was an unsung planet by any yardstick. If not for the asteroid headed its way, it'd never have made news somewhere like Satellite Five.

'Why don't you tell us about these insects?' suggested the Doctor.

Doom wondered if Kat had noticed yet that the Doctor was almost within gun-snatching range. The Lesser Order of Oberon offered a multitude of training courses for its assassins, some of whom were enthusiastically combative. Doom's preferred method of assassination was intoxication – she was often able to charm her target into befriending her, which made mickey-slipping the most straightforward route to her fee. But she wasn't entirely blind to the inherent dangers of life as a killer. Some people very badly didn't want to die and took extreme care to avoid it, as had Stalgon. Wearily, she'd therefore accepted the need for a self-defence course. Disarming an armed person who got too close was, if you put in a hundred hours of practice, surprisingly straightforward. The way the Doctor was approaching Kat, whose gun was still limply held in her right hand, Doom had to wonder. Did the Doctor also know how to swipe an attacker's gun?

'They communicate with something similar to shortwave radio. It's quite remarkable. From what we can tell, they operate as a hive mind.'

The Doctor scoffed. 'Not exactly unique.'

'Not in and of itself, perhaps. But they exist in a kind of symbiosis with their environment. They can reshape it at will. Respond to stimuli that affect it. In *minutes.*'

A deafening crack suddenly shattered the stillness of their surroundings. Through the roof of the tunnel, a chink of blue light appeared. Doom stared directly overhead into the growing fracture. Through it she glimpsed a giant slice of swirling white and blue. For a second or two she struggled to believe what she was seeing.

'That's Vassta,' the Doctor announced, grabbing Doom's hand. 'Time to run.'

# Blue Box

They must have run another fifty metres before Doom became aware of Kat yelling after them.

'Stop, stop! There's more.'

Doom pulled her hand free of the Doctor's. She stalled, watching Kat catching up.

'It's like I told you,' Kat said, panting slightly. 'The insects and the asteroid – it's a joined ecosystem. The insects detect obstacles with their radio senses. Obstacles like Vassta. They adapt the shape and trajectory of their environment. That's what's happening now. We should all leave. It's not safe. The insects might see us as a threat and attack.'

'Bit late for that,' Doom said, checking over her shoulder. She put on her helmet again. At least it'd offer some protection if the glowing cockroaches returned, which now seemed likely.

Kat placed both hands on her hips. 'Then you're leaving?' She sounded relieved.

The Doctor leaned in. 'Not a chance. Doom, get to it.'

This time, when Kat raised the weapon Doom was close enough to grab it, just as she'd been trained. Eyes widening, she stepped back. She pocketed the gun, tutting in disapproval.

'Collaborating with an assassin of the Lesser Order of Oberon. You are quite the disappointment, Doctor.' Kat's voice dripped with contempt. 'Your public relations team have done a real number on us all.'

'Someone's been telling you porky pies,' the Doctor retorted, 'because you seem to think I'm some kind of idiot.'

Doom backed off. She needed to talk to the Doctor about New Venice, get some idea of how she might track down that version of him. But it was obvious that Kat was telling the truth, at least partially. Nothing the woman had yet said seemed at odds with the evidence of her five senses. The asteroid was most definitely changing shape all around them and the ease with which she'd been able to snatch her weapon made Doom suspect that Kat had no expertise in that department.

She might have to use the opt-out clause for this job. At least this time a request to punch out without completing the mission wouldn't be rejected, leaving her on her knees, cringing before imminent death.

The Doctor spoke up. 'Doom, I'm asking nicely, finish your mission, destroy the asteroid.'

'But the insects . . . ? The cave art. I agreed to blow up a space rock, not do a genocide.'

'Use your brain. Insects can't do cave art.'

Doom shrugged. 'You don't know that. Maybe their ancestors did it.'

'Snakes? C'mon, Doom. Think! What would asteroid-belt-dwelling insects know about snakes? This story is bogus!'

Another tremor shook the tunnel, this time so intensely that all three were thrown against the walls. In the rock ceiling another chasm opened. Hurriedly, Doom reached for her spacesuit's oxygen supply. Just as the airflow resumed she heard a cry from the Doctor. Staring into the chasm she saw a blue box floating along, just beyond the surface of the asteroid.

*The Doctor's time ship.*

'It's ejected the TARDIS!' The Doctor clambered to his feet and began to scrabble up the rocky wall towards the new opening in the tunnel.

Kat picked herself up. 'I warned you. The insects saw it as a threat. And if you start laying charges around the tunnels, it'll do the same to you,' she told Doom. 'Doctor, let me help.'

Doom watched as Kat began to follow the Doctor in scaling the fissure, chimney-style. 'How're you even breathing?' she marvelled. When neither responded, she guessed there was some kind of artificial gravity keeping the atmosphere on the surface, too.

For the first time, she began to wonder. Everything had made sense so far. But while she could believe those insects generated oxygen, she couldn't see how they'd generate enough energy to increase gravity. All the air should be bleeding out of the interior and into space. The

Doctor and Kat should be suffocating. Instead they were making decent progress towards the surface, from where she could see the blue box was probably no more than a few metres away.

Tentatively, Doom removed her helmet and shouted, 'Doctor, need any more help?'

*Really hope he doesn't.*

The Doctor's reply was almost lost in the roar of another mighty crack. 'I'm going to use the TARDIS's tractor beam on the asteroid to shift its trajectory.'

A moment of silence passed. 'OK. Didn't catch if you needed the extra hand, though.'

This time there was no reply. Doom checked her timer. Forty-two minutes remained. The Doctor *might* succeed, but Vassta couldn't necessarily bank on that. Rare species or not, she needed to square her conscience with completing the mission. Because if it came down to insects versus actual people, there was no contest. Moreover, she reminded herself, she wouldn't be intentionally killing the insects. They'd be collateral damage. The double-effect principle would apply – her intention was to save the lives of millions of Vasstans. It was a worthy mission, a 'good turn', as the Doctor had said.

Doom would keep her promise to Alexyi Kadh. *Totally worth it.*

She'd have to request mission completion before any charges actually went off, obviously, or else she'd be vaporised, too. It was a standard move for timed assassinations – the Lesser Order's system could check all temporal databases and confirm the kill even if a knight hadn't directly witnessed it. Given what Kat had claimed about the insects, this mission suddenly looked much riskier than Doom had expected. What if the insects could somehow deactivate the fission spikes? She'd have to spread them widely to minimise the risk. She calculated it'd take at least thirty minutes to lay fission spikes throughout the asteroid to provide enough shredding power before it entered Vassta's atmosphere.

She reached into her bag for a fission spike. Each was the size of a plum, with spikes that emerged at the touch of a pressure stud. The spikes would adhere to any surface. The whole network of charges could be set off or disarmed remotely. Inside each was a tiny speck of fissile material with an explosive yield of a hundred tonnes.

With meticulous care, Doom positioned the first spike.

*Make asteroid go boom.*

# ROBOT

After Kat's dire warnings of the insects' potential for vengeance, Doom was extra-vigilant as she moved through the tunnels. She'd laid three more fission spikes before she spied another insect horde. As before, they seemed to be beating a direct path for her. This time she was ready with the weapon. A first jolt took out the vanguard. The rest halted. It could have been her imagination, but their fierce neon glow seemed to fade a tad. Then, as though some collective decision had been made, they rushed at her again. Doom fired another bolt. Their glow flared slightly when hit but none stopped. She turned and dashed back the way she had come, occasionally firing over her shoulder.

Somehow, the bugs had instantly adapted to the charge. Internal radio communication was one thing, but *this*? Doom had never heard of a fully organic species that was capable of such rapid adaptation. The universe was full of bizarro creatures but word tended to get around about the truly extraordinary.

In the waiting room of the clinic on Satellite Five she'd finally got round to reading the full mission brief for the Stalgon job, VM2076. Apparently Vassta was an unremarkable planet, colonised more than 400 years ago by a community of refugees from yet another remote colony, a mixed-species world of Earth humans and the surviving humanoid aliens. If their planetary system was home to such an incredibly rare and sophisticated insect species, how come it wasn't mentioned in the mission notes?

For the second time in this hour, Doom had a tingly sense that something didn't add up. This Doctor, for all his reluctance to help her fix her fundamental problem, seemed to be rightly sceptical about Kat.

Still jogging to say ahead of the moving carpet of bugs, she modified the setting on her gun and fired again. This time the giant cockroaches ground to a halt. She didn't hesitate, firing bolt after bolt until the entire cohort stilled, apart from an occasional trembling leg. She approached and with the barrel of her gun turned over one of the charred insects. The creature was intact but toasted. There was an oddly chemical tang to its singed carcass. Doom had once been hired to assassinate a particularly lax, corrupt manager of an oil refinery – the employees had clubbed together for her fee. These giant, dead cockroaches stank like that refinery.

With the hilt of her weapon she tapped on the bug's carapace until it cracked, exposing a spaghetti of plastic-coated wires and a circuit board.

'Aw, come on. Robots *again*?'

Pistol drawn, Doom straightened up, rotating slowly as she surveyed every direction for a fresh approach.

The Doctor was right. Kat's story had been a pile of nonsense. On reflection, it probably hadn't been the smartest move for the Time Lord to allow her to follow him to the TARDIS. Doom doubted Kat had any helpful intention. She pushed back the tiniest twinge of almost-guilt at the memory of having left the Doctor to it.

This asteroid was no empathetic, adaptive insect nest. The bugs were like the mandroids on Stalgon's Kraal-built simulation: sentinels guarding against potential interference. The space rock had been primed for destruction, with measures taken to prevent anyone trying to destroy or divert it. Why anyone would do that was of little interest to Doom. She'd promised Alexyi Kadh's avatar that she would destroy the asteroid, remove it as an existential threat to Vassta, and so she would.

Why Kat didn't also want to save her own world was a mystery. Doom couldn't waste time worrying about that, either. Loads of things were baffling. Avoiding having to worry about them was one of the chief reasons she'd stayed in a zero-hours contract, all-consuming and time-hopping job.

She bent down and picked up the cracked robot-insect, pulling out wires to expose the circuit board. With the right kit, she'd probably be able to trace any signal received back to its origin. It could be anywhere on the asteroid, or perhaps on a nearby spaceship. Maybe the TARDIS wasn't the only spaceship that'd parked itself?

The TARDIS could take care of itself, Doom suspected.

But anyone on board another parked ship in the vicinity would almost certainly be killed when she detonated the fission spikes. It was an unwelcome thought, but the millions of lives on Vassta were her priority.

She dropped the robot insect carcass into her backpack and continued towards the centre of the asteroid, placing fission spikes every fifty metres. A peek at the vortex manipulator's timer told her she had thirty-eight minutes left. It seemed like a lot, but she had a lot of ground to cover and further encounters with marauding cockroaches would eat severely into her remaining time.

Only six fission spikes remained in her bag by the time she reached what she guessed must be the centre. The asteroid was about a kilometre across and since leaving the Doctor near the surface she'd placed ten of the powerful but tiny bombs. She'd seen off two more attempted cockroach blitzes, leaving her staser pistol dangerously low in charge. The further she moved from the outer edge, the less impact from each shuddering shape-shift of the asteroid, which appeared to mainly affect the surface. In fact, that whole phenomenon struck Doom as some kind of movement designed to brush off anything parked near the surface. Another aspect of the asteroid's self-defence?

The more she understood it, the less the rock seemed like an asteroid belt escapee and the more like a designed projectile weapon. But why destroy the Vasstans? They were nobodies from nowhere, on a nowhere planet. Three assignments in three hours, all turning out to be somehow connected to that obscure planet.

*What am I missing?*

The tunnels near the centre curved into a spiral. Winding closer, she spotted that the energy drain on her thermal suit had increased. Could it be colder *inside* the asteroid? Doom struggled to understand how that could be. You wouldn't expect much temperature gradient across just one kilometre, not in the vacuum of space. She checked the temperature in the tunnel. It was a toasty thirty-seven degrees centigrade. No wonder her thermal suit was draining energy – it'd gone into cooling mode.

Doom took a deep breath. There had to be something hot at the centre of this asteroid. Energy was pouring off it. It was all beginning to make sense. This asteroid wasn't an escaped belt-rock that had been harnessed for its destructive power. It was powered by something hot, controlled by someone who intended to destroy Vassta.

# SHIP

Moments later, Doom found the energy source. Parked snuggly in a cavern that (according to her estimations) lay at the heart of the asteroid, was a spaceship. From its appearance, she guessed that most of the craft comprised part of a propulsion mechanism. It resembled the ship that'd smashed into the Kraal-simulated asteroid, itself a rock that must have been tractor-beamed out of orbit and sent hurtling towards whatever innocent world the Kraal simulation engineers had used as the stand-in for Vassta.

It was a remote-controlled, over-powered ship, designed to propel an asteroid. From what Doom understood, in the whole Mahd vs Kadh insanity, Kat's sympathies lay with the Mahds. According to the data ghost, Alexyi, the Kadhs had commissioned the asteroid-smasher. The Mahd faction, presumably, had commissioned *this* ship actively to attack their own world.

Doom had met some extremely messed up characters in her time, but a suicidal tendency on this scale was unprecedented. She'd believed nothing much could shock her. She'd been wrong.

*This is straight-up evil.*

The ship thrummed with energy that pulsed out of it and into the rock walls behind it. She circled the craft, watchfully. It had no obvious windows and only a tiny cabin. If someone was aboard and armed she'd be a sitting target. Yet something told her it was unmanned. Kat had evidently arrived with the Doctor. There was no sign of life on board. To the rear of the ship she saw that the propulsion section was indeed fused to the rock, as though it'd been inserted into a pre-built slot. According to the LiDAR map in her monocle tracker, it opened into a tunnel and then to empty space. She was in the engine room of the asteroid. Here then was the obvious solution to save Vassta, better even than detonating the fission spikes.

The Doctor would be able to figure out how to alter its trajectory – the advanced technology wouldn't faze him at all. Doom turned and began to run. She had twenty-one minutes remaining on the timer. She had to reach the Doctor, fast.

It took her three minutes to reach a tunnel that lay close to the surface. No insects came anywhere near her – their systems seemed designed to target anything approaching the centre, not moving away. The fissures in the rock ceiling had grown huge. The Doctor and Kat had used the chimney method of climbing to reach the surface in much narrower cracks, but these walls were wide open, like two sides of a ravine. Outside the asteroid's surface, the blue oceans and white clouds of Vassta loomed terrifyingly large. It couldn't be much longer before the asteroid entered the atmosphere, maybe even sooner than Doom's safety margin.

*Die on this rock? Don't think so.*

'Still here, are you?'

Doom whipped round, gun drawn. 'Stop right there or I'll shoot.' She hesitated just long enough to hear Kat chuckle.

'Weapon down. Nice and slow.'

The detonator was on Doom's belt. Worst-case scenario, she could afford to lose the gun.

*Could use an upgrade, truth be told.*

Carefully, she laid it on the ground to her right.

'Hands in the air again.'

Doom breathed a silent curse. She should have opted for the more expensive detonation kit with the blink-operated timer. She sensed Kat approaching from behind. After her rapid disarming of Kat half an hour earlier, the Vasstan was rightfully wary of Doom's combat ability. But when she saw Kat's hand on the staser and heard a brief sigh of relief, she realised she'd been conned.

She spun round to see Kat aiming Doom's own pistol at her – and no other weapon in sight. 'You lost your gun,' she blurted. *It's official, I'm the queen of idiots.*

'In a good cause,' Kat countered and added grudgingly, 'although, yes, I do seem to have mislaid it. But thanks for yours. Much obliged.'

Doom observed the smug expression on Kat's face. It was disconcerting how Earth-human were this Vasstan woman's expressions, nothing like the more restrained, sanguine expressions of Stalgon, Alexyi Kadh and the mandroids. Of those, only Stalgon was a real Vasstan humanoid but the other two were at least designed to mimic actual Vasstan people.

Kat, on the other hand, apart from her Vasstan olive-brown skin, honey-brown eyes and the black tattoos (or birthmarks) on her forehead and near the right ear, gave off powerful, mean, alpha-Earth-human-female vibes. Where Doom was from, such people were known as 'Janahs'. It was odd, almost as though Kat had spent enough time among Earth-humans to pick up their idiosyncrasies.

'I take it the Doctor's plan didn't work?'

Kat barked out a brief, sardonic laugh. 'Not unless his plan was suicide.'

Doom was shocked into silence. The Doctor was dead? After several seconds she said, 'He's a Time Lord, though. He'll regenerate.'

'Maybe yes, maybe no. Either way he's not going to change anything for us. Let's get back to you – why are you still here?'

Frustration built within Doom. If she could just reach her belt without Kat seeing, she could set off the timer. Even if she knew about the fission spikes, Kat would be shredded before reaching the first one.

*Set the timer for three minutes, punch out of the mission.*

It seemed like an acceptable margin. Or she could kill Kat first. She was infuriated enough to do it. This had been her best chance to talk to the Doctor, find out how to locate the version of him from the masked ball. Even though it'd been hours since Doom had last seen the cowled figure of Death approaching, the memory of its spectral image rarely left her thoughts.

'I understand,' Kat said. 'You like to be seen as the enigmatic, silent type, is that it?'

'Nah,' Doom replied airily. 'Just don't have a lot to say. Looks like you've got everything pretty much in hand.'

Kat smiled, her most human expression yet; pure smug, superior cruelty. 'I do, at that. The Doctor saw it, too. But only at the end.'

Doom wanted to kick herself. Now she remembered exactly what it was she'd missed about Kat.

# Checkmate

'How did you know I'm with the Lesser Order of Oberon?'

Doom almost never had to control the impulse to kill. Yet, at this moment, it took about half of her willpower to stop herself enacting one of the methods she'd already formulated for 'seeing off' the Vasstan woman, as the Doctor put it. The other half was engaged with maintaining an air of blithe disinterest.

If Kat truly understood anything about hitters in the Order, she'd know how ludicrously dangerous it was to threaten one physically.

*If you go for the King, better not miss.*

From the shrewd smile that spread across Kat's unusually expressive face, Doom guessed that the Vasstan might have some clue about the risk. 'A slip-up on my part,' Kat admitted. 'But to be fair to me, you took your time.'

'Noticing? Oh, I noticed,' Doom said. It was only a semi-lie.

Kat's silence and her supercilious smile suggested that she was on to Doom. But that didn't matter. In fact, it might even be helpful. Overconfidence made people sloppy.

'In case you're wondering, the Doctor didn't give you away,' said Kat.

'Very decent of you to tell me that.'

'Fair's fair. One good turn, as they say. I owed you; now we're even.'

Doom let her gaze slide over Kat's trigger finger for a fraction of a second, then took a bold step forward. People who were serious about shooting you tended to actually do it when provoked. In her experience, however, most people who took the risk of conversing with a professional killer while pointing a gun at them had little intention of firing. And Kat already knew that Doom was capable of snatching a weapon at close range; Kat would either shoot or step back.

Hesitating briefly, Kat stepped back, raising the pistol. 'Not another step.'

Doom suppressed a smile. *Gotcha.* 'So, what's the good turn I did you?'

'Can't you guess?'

'I'll take "hired me to kill someone" for five hundred, Alex.'

'Too easy. The point is, who?'

*Ugh. Can't abide time-wasters.*

'Look, I'd love to chat but I'm on a bit of a clock.'

'*Who* hired you, "Doom"?'

'Tsk, naughty. If you've used my services you'll remember the NDA part.'

Kat cocked the weapon.

*Get you, Business-Time vibes.*

'Final warning,' Kat said, her voice soft and menacing. It was a pretty convincing act. If Doom hadn't known exactly what'd happen when Kat pulled the pistol's trigger she might even have been fooled.

'Wait,' Doom urged. She tried to look scared. 'Please, don't kill me. We need each other to escape.'

Her brain went into overdrive. Kat might well be dead within seconds, deleting information that could prove crucial for Doom's survival. The last three jobs all connected to Vassta. That couldn't be a coincidence. Two of the clients had been anonymous, the third was Alexyi Kadh's avatar.

*Think.*

First, the hit on Stalgon, the designer of the simulation of an asteroid impact on Vassta, the point of which seemed to be to prove that it wouldn't be too catastrophic. This argument appeared central to the Mahd position, so it was a reasonable guess that the client who wished Stalgon dead was from the Mahd faction. However, the Kadh leader had evidently introduced an asteroid-smashing spaceship into the simulation. This made *both* factions a party to the simulation. It wasn't what Doom would expect if *either* had hired her to kill Stalgon. Murder wasn't always rational but assassinations usually were.

Second, the murder of the data ghost. Revenge for Stalgon? Maybe. But Stalgon was a Vasstan. Surely those people had bigger problems? Had the client also arranged to kill Doom, too, and the TV producer? Multiple deaths muddied the waters.

*Focus on the OG client. Cui bono from the death of the data ghost?*

Doom almost breathed it aloud. *This is about the data.* Both assignments were aimed at suppressing the results of the simulation. The client in *both* cases didn't want Vasstans to know how catastrophic the asteroid impact would be. Killing Doom and the TV producer into the bargain looked a lot like a standard witness-clearing job. Control of the narrative was the ultimate client's target.

These facts pointed to Abo Chenoute and the Mahds, who wanted nothing done to stop the asteroid.

'You're slower than I expected,' Kat remarked. She seemed to think better of her gunplay and lowered the weapon. 'I really thought you'd see it.'

'I *do* see it. You're a Mahd, and you hired me to kill Stalgon and the ghost.'

The Vasstan woman's nod was barely perceptible. 'Now tell me I'm deluded. Superstitious. A deranged follower of Abo Chenoute.'

Doom sighed. 'Mate, I wouldn't let you off that easy. "Deluded" is being certain you'll win the lottery with one ticket. Getting an asteroid to crash into your home planet, that's *horrific.*'

Kat's hollow laughter echoed. In the distance Doom heard the approach of another mighty crack as the outer wall of the asteroid began to fracture. She risked a glimpse of her timer. Seventeen minutes. This inane conversation was gobbling up valuable time.

'You humans are all alike,' Kat said. Her attempt at humour dripped away leaving only contempt. 'Pathetic. Wheedling. And *incredibly* uncomfortable. Even with full compression.' A full-throttled burp escaped her mouth. ''Scuse me,' she giggled. 'Better out than in.'

# Comms

Something peculiar was happening to Kat's face. Doom was fairly certain that when they'd first met she'd been slim in body and face, not unlike the lithe figure of a Vasstan female on which the first Mandra was based. Now Kat's cheeks seemed to be plumper and she had a double chin. It was as though she were being inflated from the inside.

If this was some horrible side effect of oxygen deprivation, it was a new one for Doom. Her own helmet was still in place – after watching giant ruptures in the outer tunnels of the asteroid she was taking no chances. Yet Kat was still breathing and she'd presumably been even closer to the surface. Doom guessed that the spaceship in the centre of the asteroid was exerting some gravitational effect on the air, which if Kat could be believed, was kept oxygen-rich by the insectoid bots.

So why was Kat's face swelling up as if she'd eaten a handful of allergenic snacks?

Doom was about to ask Kat what was wrong when another shockwave hit just below their feet. She was thrown to the ground, which promptly began to crumple and fold beneath her, pitching her towards a wall that was now two metres lower. She felt her helmet whack loud and hard against rock. Her brain seemed to wobble for a moment. Behind her eyes, a curtain of white descended.

*Must not. Close. Eyes.*

Her eyelashes fluttered as she focused all energy on staying conscious. Through narrow chinks she watched darkness fall between where she was now and where Kat had been. Even if she'd wanted to help – which she didn't – Doom doubted she'd have the strength. She wasn't even sure she could stand up.

'*And* that idiot still has my gun,' she grumbled. All that anticipation waiting to see it backfire on Kat – for nothing. She wondered if the Vasstan had guessed the pistol was configured exclusively for Doom's personal use? Probably not. Whatever had been going on with Kat those last couple of minutes could not have been comfortable. Now the Vasstan had almost certainly been crushed to death by the collapsing asteroid. If not for the helmet, Doom's head would have cracked open like an egg. Turning slightly, she groaned as a wave of pain hit. She could see no obvious way out.

Doom reached for the detonator at her belt. This was it, then. A three-minute timer and then she'd request early completion of the mission. The Doctor might be dead; Kat too, probably. No one and nothing could stop the detonation now. All she need do was set the timer and the asteroid would surely be destroyed, her assignment completed and her promise kept to the Kadhs' data ghost, young Alexyi.

Doom examined the dispatch app. Even when clients requested anonymity, Terri could gain access to their full details. No investigation was permitted unless the contract were somehow violated. Being physically threatened by a client was one of those conditions. There was a chance she could unlock a few more details about the client, if not their actual name.

She managed to pull herself up until she could lean against the tunnel wall then opened the dispatch app. The seismic tremors had subsided – for now. They seemed to arrive every seven minutes, but that might change.

She selected the Stalgon assignment. Normally she avoided taking connected missions. They tended to have connected clients too, and those connections could turn sketchy if things went wrong. Today was abnormal all round, however. Shakily, she began to complete the form required to access basic information about an anonymous client. It was her first time accessing this feature and she could tell right away; the questionnaire had a definite tang of Terri.

*Q: Why do you need more information about this client?*
*(tick all that apply)*
*Client stalked knight*
*Client threatened knight*

*Client tried to kill knight*
*Client actually killed knight (only tick this option if you are a named executor on the knight's last will and testament.)*

She ticked A, B and C, muttering, 'Happy now, Terri?'

The screen refreshed, displaying details of the organisation that had transferred payment before the contract had been accepted.

SLITHEEN, SLITHEEN & SLITHEEN, S.A.

Doom hadn't heard of the company, which she noted had been incorporated in Panama City, Earth. The date of its incorporation was truly astounding. Early twenty-first century! Slitheen, Slitheen & Slitheen, S.A. was a couple of millennia shy of 200,000 years old, registered by legal firm Fossack Monseca & Co.

Kat worked for a thoroughly ancient, private Earth company. Not a particularly enlightening detail, but rather odd given her final words: '*You humans are all alike. Pathetic. Wheedling. And incredibly uncomfortable.*' Weird thing for a Vasstan to say. As far as Doom knew, Vasstans were ninety-five per cent human, and the colony had never taken hassle from Earth. But history could be complicated. There was obviously a lot more going on with that world.

Doom prepared to set the three-minute timer on the detonator. Just before she pressed the button, it occurred to her to check the strength of any comms signal on the vortex manipulator. The Lesser Order was justifiably proud of its engineering team's innovation, which enabled the dispatch app to piggyback off the communications network of any society that had developed any kind of digital communications whatsoever. The vortex manipulator did the rest, boosting the signal and sending it through time to the Lesser Order's headquarters on Celetrial Prime.

The comms tech rarely failed, which was why it took Doom a few seconds to recognise the icon that now blinked steadily on the vortex manipulator's screen. She'd hardly ever seen it before.

There was no signal. *Nada.* Vassta had gone entirely dark, nothing to piggyback off. There was no way to punch out of this mission, completed or not. She'd have to use the old-school emergency protocol and vortex to an inhabited world with satellite technology. Unfortunately, updating the emergency protocols was a faff, a super-buggy process that the tech team on Celetrial Prime notoriously neglected, so she hadn't bothered for a while.

*Just what I wanted – a few random days bumping around an ancient civilisation's theme park.*

Either that or help Vasstans repair whatever damage had been done to their communications network – not exactly something in Doom's wheelhouse.

It was devastating news. Doom sensed the oxygen leaving her brain. A wave of nausea rose in her gullet. She only just managed to pull off the helmet before vomit hit the back of her throat. After throwing up against the wall, she wiped her mouth with the back of her hand.

Close to despair, she pressed a cheek to the rock, enjoying the cool sensation against the flushed heat of her skin. There was only one choice remaining. All the effort she'd put in today to escape death, everything had led her here, to die on the very space rock she was trying to destroy.

She could still keep her promise to Alexyi and she would save millions on Vassta. But it would be the last thing she ever did.

# CHARITY

*It must have been the lack of oxygen,* thought Doom. There was no other explanation. Two minutes earlier she'd been serenely contemplating her own extremely violent (but quick) death in an act of spectacular charity, a self-less sacrifice to save a planet of people she'd basically never met.

She had expected to feel lifted by a sensation of pure, selfless heroism. That hadn't happened. Instead she had experienced an insistent, frustrated internal voice telling her to stop being so bloody silly, *actually search* for a way out, *at least try* to remove the fission spikes nearest to the asteroid's centre and to get inside the spaceship before setting off the remaining explosives. That way there'd be an outside chance that the craft might break free with her inside and in one piece.

*Two birds, one stone.*

Grumbling, she began to hunt around more carefully,

flashing a light into every nook and cranny of the collapsed tunnel. She spotted a place where the light seemed to penetrate further and began to remove the smaller rocks. After only two minutes she'd cleared enough space to crawl inside. Once through, she slid down the heap of rocks on the other side and landed on her gloved hands. Then she took off at a swift trot, heading towards the interior. She only managed to find one of the charges she'd placed closer to the spaceship, which might give her a berth of maybe fifty metres.

It'd have to be enough.

Cautiously, Doom entered the spaceship. There was no obvious position for a pilot. The craft was probably remote-controlled, like the Kadhs' asteroid-smasher. In mounting desperation, she searched for the best place to be when she detonated the fission spikes.

It wasn't at all obvious that anyone had expected more than one-time use of this ship. Whoever planned this evidently had access to incredible levels of funding. A Kraal-simulated planet complete with totally realistic asteroid. Robotic sentinels – humanoid *and* insectoid. Two remote-controlled spaceships for single use only. Compared to all of that, two lucrative contracts for the Lesser Order of Oberon were a drop in the ocean– and they were *juicy* contracts.

It seemed absolutely deranged to spend all this money, to kill this many people and destroy the lives of so many others, all in the name of religion. More than anything, it made Doom feel deeply sad.

*Such a waste.*

Then she remembered the weirdest anomaly – the

organisation that had paid for Kat's 'juicy' contracts. Judging from the three 'Slitheen's in the name, it was probably a family company. What did an ancient Earth company founded by the 'Slitheen' family care about a religious squabble on Vassta?

A deafening and now-familiar *vworp-vworp* sound sent Doom crashing to her knees. She covered her ears. The Doctor's TARDIS was about to materialise on top of her. At the final instant it seemed to shift by half a metre, leaving her with her nose pressed against the door. When it opened, she toppled inside. Just before she hit the ground, the Doctor grabbed her at the elbows and heaved her back outside. Doom thought she caught a glimpse of a cavernous space within, rusty-brown and orange décor and a glowing green column at its centre.

The Doctor stepped out of the TARDIS. 'You all right?'

Doom gazed intently at the TARDIS. It looked to be tightly wedged into the interior of the asteroid's controlling spaceship and left barely enough room for her and the Doctor.

'Precision flying.' The Doctor beamed. 'Even managed not to squish you. Not bad, eh? Although it's down to you I knew exactly where to land inside the ship, so . . . joint effort. Fair?'

'Thought you were with Kat.'

'I wouldn't follow Kat into Starbucks.' The Doctor was already poking around, examining the ship's only control panel.

'She thinks you're dead. Well, she *did*.'

He nodded with polite disinterest.

'What are you doing?'

'Looking for evidence – the data core. Someone's behind all this, need to find out who.'

'I was about to blow up the asteroid.'

A look of panic flashed across the Doctor's face. 'Oh, no. Tell me you haven't set the detonator.'

'Almost! "Complete your mission," you said!'

'Yeah, but that was ages ago.' He grinned. 'Got a much better idea. I decided against the tractor beam. Now you've found the ship, we've got a plan B.'

Doom peered at the spaceship's control panel, watching the Doctor open a locked cover. Once he had access to the flight controls his fingers danced over the touch panel, altering the trajectory. He turned to her, triumphant. 'It's working. The ship's driving the asteroid into a new orbit. Gonna send it crashing into the sun! Now that is *how* you save the day.'

Doom consulted the vortex manipulator's timer. Four minutes left. 'How long will that take, d'you think?'

'Until it crashes into the sun? A few days. Or a week.'

'Or you could be precise,' she said. 'Down to the minute, ideally. Or I forfeit the fee.'

The Doctor's delight was replaced with a severe glare. 'Oh, right. It's all about money for you.'

'Wrong. It's about *honour*.' Doom detached the detonator and held it in her right palm. 'I can blow it up right now. Or you can tell me exactly *when* it burns in the sun.'

He tapped another button and pointed to the refreshed screen. 'See for yourself.'

Doom entered the information onto her dispatch app and punched out of the job. After a minute the 'kill' was confirmed. The message 'Donate fee to which charity?' appeared.

The Doctor gave a short, sarcastic laugh. 'Philanthropist?'

'I do my bit.' Ostentatiously, she selected 'Intergalactic Rescue'.

'If you say so. All right.' He hooked a thumb towards the TARDIS. 'You coming with?'

'What about the data core?'

The Doctor jabbed a button on the panel. A drawer opened and he removed a storage stick. 'All done.'

Seconds later, they were standing in the centre of the TARDIS – a space many times the volume of the exterior. Doom had heard that each Time Lord's craft was different, the décor tailored to the individual tastes of the owner. This one, the smiley, youngish, blue-eyed, sticky-out-eared guy in the black leather coat, seemed to enjoy a distinctly gloomy ambience. Those easy grins were probably a mask for something darker.

'Y'know,' she began, removing her radiation suit and once again donning her cloak, 'I don't get why you didn't just tractor-beam the asteroid away.'

'Couldn't leave you, could I? Not when you were about to blow it up.'

Doom turned to face him. 'Kat's dead,' she said.

The Doctor didn't reply. She guessed he already knew. If he'd found Doom, he must have some way of locating living beings near a landing site.

After a few minutes tinkering with the TARDIS controls, he spoke again. 'I reckon we should be getting going. Time for a coffee? I know just the place.'

Doom checked the app on her vortex manipulator. There were no juicy new jobs flagged for nearby time distortion but, even so, she had to pick something just to keep moving. It was anyone's guess how long before her timeline collapsed.

'I would but honestly, I don't have time.'

The Doctor guffawed and took out a hand-held tool. It didn't look like any weapon she'd ever seen. 'Really think you should. Won't take long, promise.'

# Eleven Hours

# 2006

'So this is Starbucks? Huh. I guessed a supermarket.'

'Not just any Starbucks, the original; Pike Place.' The Doctor gestured towards the rainy street beyond the window, where busy commuters hurried to work. 'Right now their "coffee culture" is catching fire, spreading all over the world.'

Doom sipped the latte and winced. 'Ugh. What's with the weird taste?'

'Cow milk. From actual cows.'

'Yuck. Anyway, explain what you did with the thingy?'

'The sonic screwdriver? I rigged your vortex manipulator to slow down that last five minutes into ten. Best I could do within the limitations but still,' he said, grinning. 'Bank holiday rates!'

Doom's hand went instantly to her timer. It was true. The hour now showed seven minutes remaining – ordering coffee had used three.

'Why would you do that? I told you; I *have* to take another mission.'

'And you will. But this'll be quick. And it's important. Look Doom, this is 2006. It's one year after the Slitheen form their company, Slitheen, Slitheen & Slitheen. And it's three months after they concoct a plan to take over the Earth. Obviously I stop them,' he added nonchalantly.

Doom simpered, 'Clever old you.' She took another sip then pushed the drink away. It tasted like an abattoir. 'How come I've never heard of them?'

'You might be surprised what else you've never heard of. Governments tend to be pretty good at hiding embarrassing episodes of their past. In this case not just Earth but the Slitheen's own people. Anyway, 2006 is when the Slitheen start playing silly beggars on Earth. When they first run into *me.*' The Doctor grimaced. 'Some folk don't realise this planet is under my protection. Most scarper when they find out. Others, I dunno. It seems to spur them on.'

'Maybe you should leave well enough alone, then,' Doom commented, tartly. 'Speaking as an Earther.'

'When I checked up on Satellite Five and saw your message to me on *Ghost v Assassin,* I also saw the news about that TV producer. Did you ever find out how he died?'

'Mutilated, apparently. I'm guessing he got too close to the bomb he hoped would kill *me.*'

'Mutilated? You could say that. All they found was "one organ". His *skin.* That sound like a bomb blast, to you?'

Doom scrutinised the Doctor's utterly deadpan expression. 'Kulekvo was skinned alive?'

'I think your producer was *already* dead. Maybe even before he commissioned the show. See, the Slitheen have a technology that allows them to inhabit the skins of their victims.'

She took a moment to absorb this. 'They're shapeshifters?'

'It's not a natural ability. They're more like high-tech cosplayers. Slitheen are Raxacoricofallapatorians.'

'From the Raxas Alliance? No way! Tall, green chappies, babyfaces with great, googly lizard eyes? They're too big!'

'Quite a bit bigger than humans,' he agreed. 'A lot of face and muscle to pack in; can lead to some gassy side effects. The latest I've run into them was on a prison planet. One of 'em was trying to track down their lost compression technology, but that was almost 200,000 years before you met yours. They've had time to improve the tech, cut down on the burping and farting.'

She tried to remember. Andre Kulekvo had shown no sign of flatulence. But Kat . . .

*'Better out than in.'*

'Kat had a bit of a moment,' Doom admitted. 'Right before she got crushed. And the Slitheen company paid for her assignment.' She fell silent. Kat had hired Doom to kill Stalgon and then the data ghost. Kat had effectively sent her to Satellite Five. 'You're right – Kat had time to organise the whole *Ghost v Assassin* thing.'

'Not "Kat". If that person was a Slitheen then I'm afraid the Vasstan woman we met was yet another victim.'

Doom frowned. 'What do they even want with Vassta?'

'Whatever it is, think big. Because they always do.'

'Oh well, I'm out. Their asteroid plan failed. Nothing to do with me, now.' She drank more latte and cringed. 'Cow's milk. Eww.'

The Doctor gave a dismissive chuckle. He took her drink and placed it on a neighbouring table. 'Right, I'm off. But don't hurry back to work. Stay here a while, drinking and eating like a local. Give it a go!' Then as if it were a mere afterthought he added, 'Slitheen were pretty big news here on Earth, three months ago. You might want to investigate.'

As the Doctor stood up to go, she grabbed his wrist. 'Wait. I still need to know how to stop . . . y'know.'

Their eyes met, his filled with renewed compassion. 'I'm trying to help, Doom. Stay. Use what time you have left.' He indicated the vortex manipulator. 'We both know using that thing won't do you any good.'

She ignored the comment. A Time Lord lording it over her method of time travel was too obvious to merit a response. 'Stay in the twenty-first century? Shouldn't I at least be with my friends?'

'Oh, you want companions for your death? People with friends like that don't usually work for the Lesser Order of Oberon, pal. Yes, the twenty-first century. That's where the Slitheen family's crimes really take off. Like I say, look into it.'

Doom held on to his arm for another second then reluctantly let go. 'What if I'm afraid?'

*He's not going to help me.*

'We're all afraid, Doom. We both know that what happened means your timeline is collapsing. I can't help with that.'

She stared. 'We both know *what,* now?' He wasn't making sense. Her problem was simple: cause and effect. Remove the cause, reverse the effect. 'What about the *you* I met on New Venice? He was *there,* he could stop it!'

The Doctor shook his head. 'And *this* me is steering well clear. Too many unforeseen consequences. You should know that better than anyone.'

Doom was too crestfallen to even watch him go. The Doctor obviously had his own issues with whatever was happening on Vassta. Why wouldn't he share more?

Shc did a speedy scan of search results for 'Slitheen' on the ancient 'Internet'. The Doctor was right – there were several headlines about their attempt to start a nuclear war on Earth for access to its raw materials. Much of it read like pure bunkum. But some details had the ring of truth.

*Facts about the Slitheen are difficult to come by, but people with credible backgrounds have seen classified documents and leaked some details.*

She blinked as an image of a Raxacoricofallapatorian would-be invader of Earth appeared on the screen, taken from footage captured on security camera. The Slitheen was weirdly cute and surprisingly hench, apart from its round belly.

*Why* had the Doctor suggested she 'look into' the Slitheen? Was he hinting at some connection between them and her collapsing timeline? When he said 'don't hurry back to work,' was that just another way of saying 'have a rest, you need it'? Was he suggesting that if she stopped killing for a living then things might improve? Or was it something more cryptic?

*As cryptic goes, "your timeline is collapsing" scores a ten.* It made no sense for her to investigate the Slitheen. The past was the past. Ultimately, did she even care who paid for her services?

Doom sighed and bade a mental goodbye to Starbucks and Earth, 2006. It seemed like a pretty cool place, retro and peaceful. But the vortex manipulator's timer – assuming the Doctor's tinkering hadn't blitzed it – showed less than three minutes left. Nothing left to do but select another mission.

Two new assignments had appeared on the dispatch app. She couldn't have ignored them if she'd tried. Both were contemporaneous *and* co-located. Twice the payday for the same hour. This was so rare that every available hitter in the order would be interested.

*Seriously, Vassta – again?*

VK3075 and VM3076. She'd finally get a chance to visit the real Vassta. But, with growing dismay, she read the headlines. This whole Vassta business didn't seem to be over, after all. It had to be why the Doctor had hinted so strongly about the Slitheen. Plus, these jobs were practically bespoke. How could she allow any other assassin to nab them?

Before she could change her mind, in rapid succession Doom selected both jobs. She speed-read instructions and with a quick nod at each fee, signed the contracts.

She got through the next minute by breathing deep and slow, trying to control her racing heart. The sensation of being in over her head was close to overwhelming. Fifty-four seconds to go. She picked up her backpack and headed for the bathroom, washed her hands and then tucked herself into a cubicle to wait.

In situations like this, Doom normally held the door closed rather than locking it. After she vortexed away a locked, empty cubicle would be a tiny anomaly. She preferred to evade small harms during time travel, at the very least to avoid being responsible for one less place for people to pee. So when she felt a yank from the other side of the door, she resisted. Both assignments would begin in less than ten seconds.

The door flung suddenly open, pulled by an implacable force. She drew breath quickly, then stopped. It was there, outside the cubicle. Less than a metre away. Its face – if there even was one – lurked in shadows, the outline wreathed by shredded edges of a cowl. She sensed the tendrils of fabric moving in and out, as though she could see its breath.

Doom's whole body went rigid with terror. 'No . . .' She sensed the familiar tug of gravity as the vortex formed at her wrist. Before she disappeared, she thought she heard a low growl, like the guttural warning cry of a demon.

When she opened her eyes she was alone in a gondola on its way down a mountain. The design of the windows, ceiling, down to the patterns of the glass and three upholstered couches arranged in a triangle, were identical to what she'd experienced in Stalgon's simulation of Vassta's mountain resort, Svoda.

Gradually, Doom relaxed. It was incredible, just like the sim. The mountains too, were identical. In a clear blue sky the sun shone overhead. Below, the slopes were deserted. There seemed to be plenty of snow, although no people to enjoy it. She settled onto one of the couches. But when she blinked, even in that momentary darkness, the vision of Death returned.

It had *found* her, even with only five 'extra' minutes. The Doctor had believed they wouldn't count, since he'd merely 'stretched' extant time on the vortex manipulator. Whatever this creature was, it couldn't be deterred even by the Doctor's hoity-toity Time Lord tricks.

*Last time I let him do anything like that.*

She distracted herself with the mission briefs. When she'd read them thoroughly, she almost laughed.

*VK3075. Kill Abo Chenoute, ruler of the Mahds of Vassta. Client: Lord D'Mitre Tannelo Kadh.*
*VM3076. Kill Queen Luudmila Kadh, monarch of the Kadhs of Vassta. Client: Lady Magdah Tannelo Mahd.*

At least these clients were willing to put names to their sketchy deeds. For once Terri had included biographical information, too. When she read it, Doom actually did laugh.

The clients were *married* to each other. D'Mitre Tannelo Kadh and Magdah Tannelo Mahd were from the noblest family of Vassta but, according to the local custom, used the factional alliance as their last name. The couple had one child, an eleven-year-old boy.

*Alexyi.*

His parents were certainly dedicated to their causes. Doom doubted that it made them any easier to get along with.

*That poor kid.*

Doom took out her pistol and checked its charge – almost back to 100 per cent. She set it to staser, replaced it and reached into her bag for her tin of Cyber-Nanites, her preferred "Mickey Finn." A pinch into any food or drink contained enough nanobots to relax the cardiac muscle so gradually that a target would fall painlessly to sleep before the tiny machines stopped their heart. If she could get either or both rulers of Vassta to sit down for a drink with her, this would be the easiest job she'd had all day.

# Keynote

At the gondola base station, it quickly became obvious that the entire resort had been cleared for a conference. Tasteful signage everywhere welcomed delegates to 'Svoda 3 – Honesty and Reconciliation'. What wasn't as obvious was why Doom's name appeared on the list of delegates.

She'd been figuring out a strategy to dispatch (not fatally) two uniformed greeters that approached the gondola as soon as its doors opened. One, a Vasstan woman, eerily mandroid in appearance but with a different tattoo, eyed a handheld device and then nodded Doom through. The other, a male, didn't have any facial markings.

*Ohhh. It's a femme thing.*

'Welcome to Svoda 3, Miz Doom.'

She hesitated. Friends (she had some, contrary to the Doctor's glib observation) were often surprised to hear that Doom was popular at parties, and not only because she was a karaoke diva. Although she suspected she was actually an introvert, she was pretty fantastic at playing an extrovert. A stroke of luck, as it turned out, because socialising was essential to her career.

It wasn't unusual for a client to play cupid and arrange the meeting between assassin and target at a party. A global conference of elites was a major step up from the usual warm wine and cheap canapes. This death-meet came with a hotel room, branded drinking cup labelled 'Svoda 3', name badge with mountain-ride privileges and the organisation Doom was alleged to represent: *Ms Doom, CEO, Corinth, Inc. Vassta.*

*Ah-ha, selling post-life existence, am I?*

The young Vasstan man who'd handed her the welcome pack looked sideways and then leaned forward, whispering, 'You're from Corinth? Life as an ethereal. How real does it feel? Be honest, remember, we're all about Honesty and Reconciliation.'

Doom raised an eyebrow. 'You mean, how real does it feel for your loved ones? Totally. They'll think they're with you, 100 per cent.'

The Vasstan greeter licked his lips nervously. 'It's quite *expensive,* though, isn't it?'

'We have various packages on offer.' She paused; they always paused. 'It depends how much post-life *you* you're prepared to gift to those you care about.'

The guy was tempted, she could tell. He looked young, he had oodles of time to save up.

*Pity I don't actually work for Corinth. I'd make one heck of a sales rep.*

'The keynote speech starts in ten minutes.' Her greeter pointed down the corridor, where Vasstan and other humanoid delegates were gathering outside two large metal doors. 'In the hall.'

'Who's the speaker?'

The greeter looked surprised until Doom managed to cover up her mistake. 'I meant to ask, who else is speaking? Obviously I know who's doing the keynote.'

'Well, yes, there are a couple of other speakers. Lady Magdah Tannelo Mahd will introduce Abo Chenoute, naturally. And Lord D'Mitre Tannelo Kadh will say a few words on behalf of—'

'The Kadh queen,' Doom interjected, with more confidence than she felt.

The greeter nodded. He peered over her shoulder, seemed eager to deal with the short line of delegates that had formed.

'I suppose the security risk of a royal visit was considered to be too high?'

Again the greeter seemed surprised, this time by Doom's naiveté. 'Of course. No Kadh monarch has visited Mahd territory since ... since I don't even know when!'

So – no easy jobs today. She'd have to kill Abo Chenoute either during the keynote or before, and then find out how to reach the Kadh queen, who might not be speaking in public but Doom knew to be there. It was super-helpful of both clients to show up in the same building.

She guessed neither knew of the other's commission, which meant she'd need to approach Lady Magdah discreetly to ask for help to locate the Vasstan woman's target, shortly after bumping off Chenoute. Not the ideal scenario for a client meeting, a high probability of this one feeling somewhat aggrieved at seeing their boss killed. Doom would have to bank on Lady Magdah being peeved enough to focus on getting her own back.

The metal doors began to open. Doom picked up her pace, aiming for a spot where the assembled crowd was still thin enough for her to sneak a place near the front.

The stage was empty, the podium lit with a single spotlight. As the audience took their seats, a discomforting vibe began to spread through the room. Judging from the expressions of puzzlement and then dismay, Doom guessed that the first speakers – her two clients – hadn't shown up.

The hall lights began to dim until the space was almost pitch black. The spotlight's intensity grew in direct proportion, until it was a dazzling column of white light. Somewhere in the darkened recess of the stage, something large and clumsy shuffled noisily towards the podium. As the shuffler stepped into the spotlight, the hall filled with gasps and a few screams.

From the anxiety and commotion, Doom guessed that few in the room recognised the alien.

A Raxacoricofallapatorian was basking in the spotlight, its two muscular green arms at rest, each ending with a fearsome triad of talons. From a weirdly babyish face with a petite, upturned mouth and rosy cheeks, solid-black eyes blinked slowly, a nictitating membrane flickering into view with each blink. The audience grew quieter as it became clear the alien had no immediate plans to attack but was waiting to address them.

Doom used the hesitation to reach stealthily for her pistol. When a target was protected by high security, the client had to supply coordinates to guarantee that a hitter would arrive inside any weapons-free zone. This meant that only she would be armed, other than all uniformed and plain-clothes security guards. At an event like this, that could easily be a dozen people.

*This could get very bumpy, very fast.*

'People of Vassta, I thank you for your attention.' The Raxacoricofallapatorian's head wobbled slightly from side to side as it spoke. Its voice sounded reasonable, female and humanoid. 'Most regrettably, I bring you sad tidings. Your leader – if you're a Mahd that is – Abo Chenoute is dead.'

Cries went up, shock and indignation. The Raxacoricofallapatorian silenced them with an impatient wave of one massive, clawed hand.

'Can't be helped, I'm afraid. What do you expect, after he encouraged global suicide?'

Doom gripped her staser gun and began to weave through the crowd towards the nearest exit. Their initial bewilderment was giving way to anger.

'There's another thing,' continued the alien. 'Won't be much easier to hear, but it must be said. Queen Luudmila of the Kadhs, she's dead, too.'

The audience erupted.

# GRIFT

Doom looked around, perplexed. There didn't seem to be much emotional middle ground for Vasstans.

*They're either aloof cucumbers or raging hornets.*

'Fair is fair,' objected the Raxacoricofallapatorian at the podium, a second before several audience members launched Svoda 3 drinking cups at her head. Over the next minute while the air filled with cries of 'Murderer!' the alien batted away projectiles, then turned her ire onto random audience members near the front. Lifting a Vasstan by the throat until the poor guy managed to eke out a squeal of panic, the Raxacoricofallapatorian brandished her victim.

'Don't be fools! Did I say I had anything to do with your leaders' deaths? I'm here to help. Aren't you supposed to be this planet's brightest and best?'

Doom resisted the urge to scoff. A gathering in a fancy resort that claimed to represent any society's 'brightest and best' struck her as likely to be the exact opposite. The mere fact that they were so ready to swallow – without proof – this alien's claim that their leaders were both dead, made her doubly sure these folk were ordinarily daft.

The tumult subsided. An aggressive voice called out, 'Get on with it, babyface. We haven't got all day.' Hundreds grumbled in agreement.

The Raxacoricofallapatorian put down the Vasstan and fussily returned to the podium. 'I am Draja Fel-Fotch Heppen-Bar Slitheen from the planet Raxacoricofallapatorius. Your leaders were executed on the orders of a temporal tribunal. Both were found guilty of stochastic terroristic opportunism.'

She paused as various people yelled over her, mostly asking her to explain 'stochastic terroristic opportunism'.

'Ignorance of the law is no excuse. It means, as should be obvious, use by any world leader of an opportunity to create stochastic terror among their population. In this case, your Abo Chenoute and Luudmila Kadh used the unfortunate imminent asteroid impact to sow discord and violence among the people of Vassta. Thanks to *our* intervention, the asteroid was diverted but, my dear Vasstans, those responsible for the crisis in your society *must* be held to account!'

'That's what this conference is about,' shouted a woman. 'Honesty and reconciliation.'

'Which sounds very worthy,' replied Draja Fel-Fotch Heppen-Bar Slitheen, with a hint of a sneer. 'Yet in the experience of the temporal tribunal it usually leads to those responsible escaping accountability. That's when we step in.'

'We've never heard of you!' yelled back the previous speaker, to a huge chorus of 'That's right!'

Doom had seen enough. This green-skinned alien was a confessed Slitheen and, according to the Doctor, most likely a criminal. There *was* no 'temporal tribunal', unless the alien meant the Time Lords, and Doom knew no history of Gallifrey working with Raxacoricofallapatorians. She couldn't tell what was really going on here, but it stank of *grift*. Turning away from prying eyes, she popped her monocle tracker into place and activated it.

Almost at the exit, she studied the audience until she'd identified ten individuals who were almost certainly carrying weapons. Their gazes roamed everywhere *except* the stage, all scanning the audience. At least two clocked her watching them before she was able quickly to switch her focus back to the stage like a normie. One wasn't fooled. He kept his eyes trained on Doom, forcing her to re-evaluate her plan. If she left now, he'd be suspicious, maybe enough to alert the rest of the security team.

All ten suspicious security guards she'd spotted could be aliens in disguise. If it was true that the Mahd and Kadh leaders were dead, then the Slitheen might have killed at least twelve Vasstans already. A Slitheen-owned company had paid for the assassination of Stalgon and the data ghost – it had to be because they wanted to protect the secret of the asteroid's certain devastation of Vassta. Now this 'Draja' character was lying to the conference delegates, falsely claiming that Raxacoricofallapatorians were Vassta's saviours.

Everything was connected to some massive grift. But what? Frustrated, Doom realised again that she really ought to have investigated the Slitheen, as the Doctor had suggested.

*Why so cryptic with your feedback, Doctor?*

'Vasstans, I wish I had better news. But for *you* there is hope!'

The disguised security team, Doom noticed, were quietly shushing objections, steering the crowd towards calm.

'Your leaders stirred up discord, it's true. They turned you against each other. So sad! Hindsight is such a valuable lens though, don't you agree? Had you known before what you know now – that Abo Chenoute and Queen Luudmila sold you out to your enemies – would you not wish them punished? Would you not wish for yourself and your families a safe haven from the calamity those fake leaders chose to bring on their own followers?'

At the words 'safe haven', the audience pricked up its ears. And the beady-eyed security guard that had been watching Doom had finally let his attention wander. She ducked below head height and squirmed the final few metres to the exit, dodging the occasional delegates who bothered to notice her unusual movement.

'That's right,' continued Draja Slitheen. 'I said "safe haven". The future of Vassta I'm afraid, is anything but secure, despite our best efforts. We are here to offer new lives off-world to all of you. Every delegate at Svoda 3 and your families, too.'

Doom cracked open a fire exit and snuck through. The tracker had now completed its map of the conference centre. Both targets now registered as moving around on the upper floors. She had maybe ten seconds before the disguised security guard noticed she'd gone. Ten seconds to get out of the hall and figure out what scam these Slitheen were running.

*'Think big,'* echoed the Doctor's warning. *'Because they always do.'*

# SUCKERS

*'What do you mean?'*

*'Why's our future not secure?'*

*'What on Vassta is it talking about?'*

From outside, Doom could hear confusion in the delegates' voices. When she looked through the huge exterior window that flanked the conference centre's lobby, she began to understand.

The sky had clouded over. The mountain opposite, which in Stalgon's simulation had contained ice tunnels, train and a secret spaceport, appeared to be crumbling from the top. It was an incredible sight, almost incomprehensible. At the peak, giant boulders appeared to be breaking off and levitating, rising slowly into the atmosphere. Before her eyes, thousands of tons of rock were disintegrating. She followed the trail of enormous, levitating crumbs of mountain. Behind a cloud she caught a glimpse of a hovering, cylindrical vessel. Doom's veins chilled.

*Ore suckers!*

She'd once been hired to assassinate a mine owner who'd laid off his entire workforce in favour of ore suckers. Highly automated, one ore sucker could replace ten ground-based miners and also expensive mining hardware – each vessel needed only a pilot who also operated the "crumber".

*So. The Slitheen are mining Vassta.*

Ore suckers were certainly efficient in comparison with human power, but they were a disaster for the environment, even worse than regular mining. No responsible government would allow ore suckers to operate anywhere within 200 miles of a populated area.

The situation was becoming clearer. The asteroid was an attempt to break up part of the planet – presumably where the ore was located – and use the natural disaster as a cover. The Mahds seemed to be in favour of letting the asteroid hit their world. Perhaps they were in on the scam. They'd tried to kill Stalgon, then the data ghost carrying evidence from his asteroid-crash simulation.

Doom suspected the Slitheen would turn out to be unreliable business partners. This had to be why they had killed both Mahd and Kadh leaders. Yet it still didn't make sense. Surely the Vasstans would simply appoint successors?

*From where? They're offering all the elites a way out.*

Draja Slitheen was busily trying to remove potential opposition among the Vasstan elite by claiming both the world's leaders were no more. Of course, both captains had to be dead if passengers were to leave a sinking ship. And like any artful grifter, Draja had shown no proof.

*Smoke and mirrors.*

From inside the hall she heard people getting ready to exit. Hurriedly she escaped into a nearby office, where she consulted the vortex manipulator's dispatch app. Both jobs VK3075 and VM3076 showed as "live" and both targets registered on the tracker. Abo Chenoute and Queen Luudmila were *still alive* – at least until Doom killed them and claimed the fees. But then she'd be helping the Slitheen.

This was why she didn't like working with governments. There was *always* a hidden agenda. She was about to leave the office when she heard the corridor suddenly alive with voices as delegates poured out of the hall.

She cracked open the door. Loud-talking Vasstans had gathered and were insisting on information about the 'deals' they'd accepted. A few were asking what would happen to those inside, who'd apparently refused the deal.

The Slitheen was moving among them, shaking hands with one huge talon and charming her new friends. Then some of the delegates noticed the crumbling mountain. The mood suddenly changed.

'It's terribly sad,' Draja Slitheen agreed soothingly. 'Some sort of gravitational phenomenon. We think the near-miss from the asteroid set off some seismic event. That's why we are helping. It's too dangerous to stay! This way to your lifeboats. Your fellow Vasstans? Don't worry, we believe they'll come around. We're very concerned about their safety.'

Doom waited until the hundred or so Vasstans who'd taken the deal had been led away.

*Bunch of idiots. Skinsuits by the end of today, the lot of them.*

When all was quiet again, she headed for the emergency staircase to an office suite on the first floor, where the tracker showed Chenoute was stationary. When she reached the corridor, she heard and saw that floor was also deserted. All four doors to the suites were open. Doom drew her gun and approached, moving noiselessly towards the sound of Chenoute's voice.

'... and still the Kadhs continue to hunt for any opportunity to strike the Mahds. How sad, my dear friends, to exist among such envy and bitterness! Alas, the Kadhs cannot abide the existence of our great Mahd nation with such resources, natural wealth and a people who will never submit to their despotic, faithless rule. Alas, for their wickedness, all Vassta now suffers the just punishment of Fate. Therefore I urge you to this most solemn and terrible conclusion: we cannot co-exist because *they* will not allow it. When your very existence is under threat, you *must* fight. Fight, my friends, or lose yourselves for ever.'

Doom stepped into the doorway. Chenoute was alone in the room, standing before a recording device. When he spotted her, he raised his hands in alarm.

'And now comes one of them to destroy me. I warned you, my friends!'

She shot him twice, in both knees. He fell to the floor, screaming. Doom approached, aiming her weapon at his head. In his eyes she saw fear and incomprehension replaced with a cunning, feral gaze. A trembling Chenoute appeared to draw a line across his forehead. There was a wet, slooping sound and then a deep, throaty chuckle as another Raxacoricofallapatorian shucked off its human skin, stretching and groaning as it emerged.

# HATE

Chenoute's remains made a grisly sight, his face and scalp split open and hanging from the Slitheen's green-skinned hip. Staring straight into the alien's nictitating black eyes, she adjusted her weapon's setting to "lethal".

'Blame my itchy finger,' she quipped. 'It's been a while since I killed a real villain.'

'You came for Abo Chenoute?' simpered the Raxacoricofallapatorian. 'That's so, so precious. But you're too late. I've already sent the message. Millions will be viewing it, right now, watching evidence of the very crime for which he was executed. Now, m'dear, wouldn't it be better for you to take a cut of the profits?'

'A cut of your scam on a whole world? There you go, mistaking me for a common criminal.'

The alien thundered with laughter. It stepped out of the remaining Vasstan skin, kicking it off as if it were a stinky old shoe. 'You Lesser Order types, calling yourselves "knights". Welcome to reality, Miz Doom. Oh yes, I know who *you* are.'

Doom cringed at his use of 'knights'. He was right, it was pretentious. Yet, even as a 'hitter', she felt bound by the Order's code. Her aim faltered. The contract was for Chenoute, not this Raxacoricofallapatorian, whoever he was. Disgusting as the alien's actions were, her business was with a Mahd and a Kadh noble.

'My name is Ecktosca Fel-Fotch Heppen-Bar Slitheen,' he continued, smoothly, 'and my spies tell me you've already met my daughter, Draja? She's terribly clever – this was all her idea, you know.' He indicated the large meeting table on the other side of the suite. 'Take a seat, enjoy some refreshment. You can't stop anything, now. Look, m'dear, why don't you claim Chenoute's kill? It's on us.'

Tight-lipped, she punched out on assignment VK3075. The vortex manipulator's timer showed twenty-six minutes remaining to assassinate Luudmila. The Kadh queen was probably already dead, though, like Chenoute, whose death-by-Slitheen was apparently not registered on the Order's timeline or else he wouldn't have shown as a live target. Another Raxacoricofallapatorian had almost certainly taken Luudmila's place.

*Most likely creating their own stupid hate-message.*

It wasn't honourable to accept the fee for a death one hadn't personally arranged. Sometimes Doom could justify it, as with Chenoute or the data ghost, when she was the first to confirm a death she would otherwise have caused. She needed to do the same with Luudmila Kadh.

*Maybe this Slitheen knows where I can find her?*

Doom holstered the pistol and approached the table. Ecktosca Slitheen touched a button on his side of the table and a coffee service rose from the centre, along with a plate of cookies.

'Indulge yourself, Miz Doom. These people know their baked goods. Made from a local groundnut, very tasty. Go ahead.'

She nibbled a cookie. 'How long have you been "Chenoute"?'

'Oh, barely five days. Best to leave such things until the last minute. Someone close to the target invariably gets suspicious. I suspect that's why your services were engaged. Chenoute always had demagogic tendencies, but since he and I became, ahem, acquainted, so to speak, he's turned everything up to eleventeen. Similarly, Queen Luudmila of the Kadhs. Do you know, she's never spoken out publicly? Ha! The Mahds are going to howl for blood when they hear her "confession".'

Without moving her head, Doom surveyed the office. This Raxacoricofallapatorian could be dead in two seconds if she chose, plus any others that dared broach the door. Ecktosca obviously knew that, hence the obsequious behaviour.

'So – you tried to use an asteroid to blow up part of Vassta to get at the ore. When that didn't work, you decided to distract the planet with a civil war, while your machine scoops up ore-containing rocks in the atmosphere.'

The Slitheen shook his head in vigorous denial. 'Dear me, *no*! Not us! Global terror? My family doesn't do things like that any longer. What a simply dreadful thing to suggest! Our *client* did those terrible things. For abzantium. You'll recognise the name, I'm sure? From our little misadventure on Satellite Five?' He watched realisation hit Doom. 'Aha, the penny drops! Guilty as charged, m'lud. I did rather enjoy being your television producer. Such gratifying mannerisms. And the kilt! What a sense of humour you humans have, what a deliciously tawdry show. Incidentally, you've no idea how *stricken* we were that we couldn't find a way to have you sing in that elevator.'

'All this . . . was for abzantium?'

'Vassta is a *quality* extraction point for abzantium. Which is terribly useful in the construction of battle armour. Instruments of defence, m'dear! How can anyone object to *defence*? We Slitheen are simply brokers. Facilitators. Just like you.'

Deep inside her chest, Doom felt rage build.

'*We* didn't commission an asteroid simulation to deceive their fellow Vasstans. Nor did our client. That was all Abo Chenoute Mahd. We advised our client to destroy the evidence, naturally. That's where you came in.'

'But you Slitheen paid for that job.'

'Through our shell company. Our client is paying top rate for anonymity. True anonymity, unlike your Lesser Order's apparently worthless guarantee. Unfortunately, it appears the Mahds *were* likely to change their minds about the asteroid, once they understood how devastating the impact would be. But now, thanks to our client's inspired intervention, the entire population will be at each other's throats. Far too busy to worry about a spot of ore-sucking.'

'Why'd you pay off the people downstairs?'

'Only the cowards. Those who would opt out of fighting for their world, if offered an easy way out.'

Doom shook her head. 'You mean, the potential peacemakers.'

Ecktosca gave a nonchalant shrug.

What did the Slitheen have planned for the majority of dissenters still in the conference hall? Were those Vasstans first to hear the hate-stirring, anti-Kadh speech she'd watched Ecktosca record? The scope and sheer cynicism of the Slitheen's plan was chilling and, Doom had to admit, impressive. She'd been wrong to accept so easily that the Mahds were ideologically blind enough to welcome their world's destruction. Whoever had decided to weaponise the Mahds' faith to make all of Vassta believe this was as ruthless as they were cruel.

'"Stochastic terroristic opportunism"? You literally accused the Mahd and Kadh leaders of the very thing the Slitheen are actually doing.'

'Have I been naughty?' Ecktosca sniggered. 'Oops. I really must—' The Slitheen broke off and turned his head, suddenly distracted.

A second later Doom heard it too: *Vworp vworp.*

# Doctor

Ecktosca's eye nictitations doubled. He spun about, desperately seeking whatever was making this alarming sound.

Doom perched casually on the nearest chair and checked the dispatch app. VK3075 was 'completed' and also 'paid'. VK3076 still showed as 'live', but was now flagged for temporal distortion. She startled.

*Hang on, was that one flagged all along?*

She couldn't remember particularly noticing that status – two co-located jobs popped up too rarely to waste time dithering. By the time she looked up again, the blue box had finished materialising in the corner of the suite, to the right of the Raxacoricofallapatorian.

*Hello, Doctor!*

Doom stood up, brushing down her jacket. For once she'd waste no time getting to the point: would *this*

Doctor help? She wasn't sure her nerves would survive one more encounter with 'Death'.

*Better not be Ol' Blue Eyes, again.*

But when the TARDIS door opened and Stalgon stepped out, she slumped back into the chair. Luckily, he didn't once look in her direction. Instead, he went straight for the Slitheen.

She fumbled for her weapon and aimed it at Stalgon's head. Then she lowered it. She'd already been paid for his assassination, which meant the kill was temporally confirmed. Was this an ethereal, post-death version of him? Or perhaps an earlier Stalgon, from before the simulation? He was travelling in the TARDIS, after all.

The Slitheen stuck out its chin and roared. It swung a claw at Stalgon. Stalgon, however, seemed unbothered. He batted off the blows as though they were affectionate jabs and kept on, in relentless pursuit until the Raxacoricofallapatorian backed off then turned and loped towards the door.

Doom was as much amused as surprised. A second figure emerged from the TARDIS. Not the Time Lord she knew but then again, he was a bit of a shapeshifter, too.

'All right, Doctor? We must stop meeting like this.' Her lips twitched in an ironic grin. 'Bet you never hear that.'

The 'new' Doctor turned to her, curious, if oblivious. He was shorter, older and more shambolic than the previous two she'd met. He had on a shabby frock coat worn over a grubby-looking shirt, cock-eyed bowtie and baggy, plaid trousers held up with braces.

His face looked rather sweet, like a mischievous boy, but was wreathed in the lines of a life well-lived. His dark hair was shaggy and unkempt with a heavy fringe, a style that went in and out of fashion on Earth – Doom had known at least five epochs that had been mad for it.

He turned to her, eyes narrowing in concentration. 'Ah yes, I remember you. The other one wrote about you in his diary. Doomsday. No, *Miz Doom*. That's you.'

Doom stepped forwards. '*Who* wrote in his diary? The Doctor?'

'Yes, the Doctor who wrote in his diary. I met you once, when I was him.' He paused, frowning. 'It can be confusing.'

'But we've met since then. You don't remember?'

His expression transformed, instantly stern and rigid as he clapped both hands to his ears. 'Stop! Not another word.' Then just as swiftly he appeared to relax and flipped a thumb in the direction of the door. 'You wouldn't happen know to where they've gone?'

'Stalgon and the Raxacoricofallapatorian?'

'Ah, you know Stalgon? And the . . . ?'

'Alien? From Raxacoricofallapatorius. Calls himself Ecktosca.'

Absentmindedly, the Doctor nodded. He examined the recording equipment that the Slitheen had just been using.

'Doctor, what are you doing here?'

'I'm here on, ah, Agency business. You understand the principle, don't you?'

'Agency? A Time Lord for hire now? Rent-a-Lord?'

A stormy darkness crossed his face. Severely, he replied, 'My own people sent me. Events on this world lead inexorably to a temporal aberration that . . . well. It wouldn't be good news for the wider universe.'

Doom wrinkled her nose. 'Nice to know someone's keeping score.'

The Doctor's expression had grown sadder. 'Most Time Lords like to watch events. Some like to intervene. And I'm afraid some like to watch those who intervene and, er, make use of them.'

'By sending them to Vassta? Doctor, it's a backwater! You sure you have the right planet?'

The Doctor glowered in silence, his lips pressed together in a firm line.

'At least tell me what you're doing with Stalgon? Me and him, we have, ah, a bit of history.'

'Stalgon supplied intelligence about the involvement of Raxacoricofallapatorians. That is all I know. And as you have correctly guessed, I cannot be more specific about my mission.'

Doom rolled her eyes. 'Fine. Be that way.'

She paused to check her timer. Twenty-two minutes left. Queen Luudmila was almost certainly dead. Doom could spend the remaining time with this Doctor and still claim the kill. He wasn't the Doctor she'd met on New Venice, but she had a hunch he was the very next regeneration.

*Time to leave. Death is literally showing up at my door. It's no time to get involved in foreign politics.*

Less than an hour ago, the vortex manipulator had saved her. Yet in the end, luck always ran out. And the memory of Alexyi Kadh's avatar wouldn't leave her, nor what he'd said.

*'He wants to see me grow up. To see all children of Vassta grow up, to have a whole planet, to escape the delusion of the Mahds. Vassta should be cared for, protected, not be destroyed . . .'*

She puffed out a lengthy sigh. 'All right, I'll help. Leave the Raxacoricofallapatorian to Stalgon, wherever he is in his timeline. Not sure why, but Ecktosca seems scared of him.'

The Doctor's eyebrows lifted. 'Well, Stalgon *is* rather angry.'

'Yeah, I picked up on that. We should find Queen Luudmila. Or rather, the alien that's killed and impersonating her. It's probably recording another pot-stirring hate-fest. If that goes viral . . .' Doom winced. 'Won't be pretty. At this point, all of Vassta is one massive can of irate worms.'

The Doctor waved her forward. 'Then we'd better hurry, hadn't we?' he said, following Doom through the door.

This Doctor wasn't like the others. Doom wouldn't have tagged him for the same Time Lord. The other regenerations all betrayed a somewhat imperious confidence, however much they disguised it with bumbling humour or winning smiles. Although she'd glimpsed the stern know-it-all she'd previously encountered, this one seemed mostly to operate in 'charming tramp' mode. Also he appeared to know nothing of their subsequent path-crossings with the Slitheen.

*Hasn't lived them, yet.*

So why was past-Stalgon getting involved? The last

Doctor, Ol' Blue Eyes, had told her he wouldn't fix problems in a person's own history.

*'Too many unforeseen consequences. You should know that better than anyone.'*

*'You should know . . .'* Why had the Doctor said that? Why suggest that she research the Slitheen? Had he been quietly preparing her for this encounter on Vassta?

It hit her like a thunderbolt. *This* Doctor's secret mission, including meeting Doom, was in *that* Doctor's past. Ol' Blue Eyes had hinted at it almost in the first thing he'd said to her. Finally she understood his enigmatic statement.

*'Time travel can be like finding a diary of your early life – you remember parts of the story but not the peripherals. Nice to meet you, peripheral!'*

# PRISONER

On the first floor was a balcony that overlooked the conference centre's lobby and entrance to the hall. By the time Doom and the Doctor reached it, she knew they were too late. From inside the hall, screams of pain and aggressive shouting were easily heard above a rhythmic battering of the entrance. In the exterior corridor, three uniformed security guards were comfortably bracing the doors with their backs. No three humans could be so strong – they had to be Slitheen imposters.

An anxious Doctor glanced at Doom. 'We have to talk to them. We must find the central communication system.'

'You do that. I'm off to see Queen Luudmila. Reckon there's an alien wearing her skin.'

The Doctor took a moment, his brow creased in deliberation. Then with conviction he declared, 'In that case you must expose the imposter.'

'You're right. Can you set the communication system to broadcast across the whole planet?'

He looked mildly offended. 'Naturally.'

'I don't have an extra gun,' she said, reaching for her bag. 'But I can sort you out with some fission spikes.'

Backing away, the Doctor glared. 'There's quite enough violence here already.'

'Sorry, force of habit. Comes with the job description.'

Doom split off in the opposite direction, towards the top-floor restaurant where her second target had been tracked. Minutes later she was gently pushing aside the swing doors to see a room flooded with natural light from expansive windows. From within she heard small noises, a few hems and haws as a woman chattered, apparently to herself.

'This bit goes *here* and this part goes *there*. Much better. Now – play message.'

*'My dear subjects of Kadh . . .'*

The Slitheen-Kadh was editing the queen's 'confession'! Doom might have mere seconds before the alien broadcast it. She put away her pistol. This required diplomacy.

She stepped into the room, beaming and waving. 'Your Majesty! You're alive! Wow, what a relief!'

In obvious panic, Slitheen-Luudmila jolted in her seat. Appearing as a Vasstan woman in her early sixties, she had on a flowing jade-green evening gown. On her head was a tasteful, bejewelled tiara. She seemed dressed for a fancy gala dinner. In the restaurant, long wooden dining tables were set with blue glass plates and fluted wineglasses, flanked with gleaming metal cutlery and adorned with bouquets of white and green flowers.

'Guards!' Then, abruptly, the 'queen' became coy. 'I meant to say, who are you?'

Doom grinned her most winning grin and laid one hand on her chest, feigning a gasp. 'My gosh! We've been so worried. It's pandemonium down there, Your Maj. Your people need you!'

A glassy smile oozed across the imposter's face. 'Quite. Thank you. And you would be . . . ?'

Doom plucked at her Svoda 3 badge. 'I'm Cressi Doom. CEO of Corinth, Inc on Vassta. They sent me to find you. Where's your security detail?'

The line of questioning was working – the imposter looked confused and flustered. 'Exactly; where?'

Doom moved forward. Slitheen-Luudmila's hand was dangerously close to the recording device controls. 'How dare they leave you! Is there anything I can do, Your Majesty?'

Suspicion flickered in the imposter's eyes. She reached for the controls. Doom whipped out her pistol and blasted the 'queen's' hand. The charge was enough to deliver a nasty burn and the imposter howled in agony, the pain enough to trigger the inner Slitheen's rage.

As the alien began to emerge from Luudmila's skin, Doom rushed closer, before its powerful talons could be freed. On the recording device she tapped a button that looked like it might be the 'broadcast' control, ducking as the Slitheen aimed a swipe at her head. Scooting away she hurled herself at the floor, flapping the edges of her cloak for added distraction as she rolled. She fired two charges at the Slitheen, which snarled with fury and launched itself at Doom, a giant leap powered by its muscular thighs.

Doom scrambled under a long dining table, crawling fast on hands and knees as the enraged alien tossed chairs across the room and dragged the table, sending plates, glasses, cutlery and flowers crashing to the floor in all directions. She was on the point of being exposed when a humanoid hand appeared under the table and grabbed her cloak.

She froze.

'Hurry,' said a man's voice. 'I know a way out.'

She reached for his outstretched hand. With astonishing ease, he hauled her out.

*Stalgon.*

This was no ethereal – they could barely push a button. It *had* to be pre-assassination Stalgon; a guy with no reason to have issues with Doom.

Stalgon yanked at her hand, pulling her towards the kitchen. They were followed by the surprisingly nimble Slitheen, which leapt onto and across work surfaces in pursuit. Stalgon abandoned Doom for a second, jumped over a worktop to distract the alien, who doubled back after him. Before she'd properly registered that she was alone, Stalgon was already back at her side. Darting between ovens and dishwashers, Doom and Stalgon scurried away only metres ahead of the alien. They flung themselves through the exit, closing a door on the Slitheen's outstretched talon. Doom stasered its hand again. From inside came loud shrieks as it snatched the limb away.

She helped Stalgon to hold the door closed while he reprogrammed the locking mechanism with his free hand. Casually, he stood back. 'I locked the only other exit. Draja Slitheen is our prisoner.'

'Wow. Nice going, Stal!'

They trotted to the elevators and took the first one to the ground floor. Doom allowed herself properly to look at Stalgon, a man who'd later die at her hands. The Vasstan appeared utterly unflustered. An ominous sensation crept over her. There was something not-right about him.

'You . . . you *are* with the Doctor, aren't you?'

Stalgon nodded, once. He fixed her with a penetrating gaze. Now Doom knew she wasn't imagining it. Every instinct told her this was no Vasstan. Uneasily, she recalled what this Doctor had told her.

*'Stalgon supplied intelligence about the involvement of the Raxacoricofallapatorians.'*

Stalgon had known there was a hit on him – that much was obvious from the horde of mandroid bodyguards he'd commissioned within the simulation. Had he also discovered that the Slitheen company paid for the hit?

'Where . . . where did you meet him?'

Stalgon didn't react to this but instead placed a hand over the elevator's controls. 'Why did you kill me?'

Doom inhaled, shakily. Her thoughts whirled.

'I know you did it. You're not an easy person to find, Miz Doom. But I've had plenty of time, thanks to the Doctor.'

'Stalgon . . . ? But you . . . you're not dead.'

'I very much *am* dead. Because you killed me. My two children – my *bereaved* children – discovered that Ecktosca Slitheen's family paid you to do it. And they had this unit created to petition the Time Lords for justice. Now you are *my* prisoner. Now *you* will pay.'

Doom gazed in horror as 'Stalgon' removed his face to reveal the same mandroid mechanism as she'd seen on the child-android in the simulation, the same inner workings behind the face of every Mandra.

Her mind went blank. All she could focus on was the background noise, which was barely loud enough to hear. Then she realised: it was a recording of Queen Luudmila's voice being broadcast around the building.

*'And so, people of the Kadh Kingdom, I implore you. Most regrettably, the Mahds leave us only one way out. They colluded with enemies of Vassta to exploit our world's natural resources. They used their traditions of faith to whip up a frenzy of hate against us. For the good of any survivor of the coming cataclysm, the Mahds must be wiped out.'*

Doom turned to him, urgently. 'You're Vasstan? A Stalgon mandroid, I get that. But whoever sent you is of Vassta, right? You must be programmed to care about what's happening out there. Aren't problems of an entire planet a teentsy bit bigger than one measly revenge-gig?'

The android stalled.

'Could you . . . pop your face back on? I'm in the death business myself, as you know. Nothing wrong with making someone's final moments more cheerful.'

Mandroid-Stalgon did as she asked. He looked bewildered. It struck Doom that whoever had programmed it hadn't made the kill-instructions clear enough. There appeared to be another, possibly higher imperative.

She indicated her drawn pistol. 'Yeah, there actually *can* be something wrong with making the final moments easier. Careful with that; it gives your target time to change their tactics. Like, I just switched *this* to "lethal".'

The android blinked. 'Not to me. Your weapon will eventually run out of charge. Then I will crush you.'

Doom fired a staser and watched him fall. 'Your mistake, Mandro.'

She had a way out – the vortex manipulator. She'd witnessed Luudmila's discarded skin, which meant the real queen was dead. Doom could punch out of VM3076, job done. The Doctor could handle the situation, now.

*Or I can stay to help save Vassta.*

Doom gazed at the downed android of Stalgon. It was too bad such a powerful creature wasn't on their side. Maybe the Doctor could reprogram it?

# H&R

Androids in the simulation had taken three minutes to revive after each 'lethal' staser charge. If Doom didn't get out of the elevator soon, she knew mandroid-Stalgon would make good on his crushing promise. With scant hope, she stabbed a few buttons on the control panel. But nothing. The android had evidently disabled the system.

She glanced fearfully at the ceiling.

*Another hatch? Come on!*

She heaved the android for several long minutes. This one was substantially weightier than the mandroids in the simulation. No wonder it had been able to fight off the Slitheen. Eventually, she managed to position it below the ceiling hatch. It was no good. This wasn't a cramped, space-saving space-station elevator; like everything else in the conference centre it was spacious, tastefully designed and deluxe. Even standing on top of the fallen android, she couldn't reach the opening.

She prepared to staser the android again when it revived.

*Stuck in here while the Kadhs and Mahds tear each other apart. Unless the Doctor managed to activate the global broadcast in time . . .*

In which case there was a chance the whole planet had witnessed the appearance of the Raxacoricofallapatorian who'd killed and stolen the Kadh queen's skin. Would people believe it was real? Conspiracies could take a fierce hold in the minds of people trained to hate.

Was it already too late for Vassta?

She began thumping the doors, bellowing at the top of her lungs. After four minutes, she shot the Stalgon android again. Her face was flushed and she was damp with sweat after four solid minutes of hollering and thumping. Where was the Doctor?

Another minute passed. Then, over the sound of her own tired yells and fist-thumping, she heard a voice from the ceiling. The hatch was open.

The Doctor's face appeared. 'Ah, so *this* is where you've been hiding.'

Exhausted, she pointed at the android. 'Any chance you could reprogram Stal here *not* to crack my skull?'

The Doctor was already lowering herself into the elevator. He knelt over Stalgon and carefully removed the face. He turned to her, eyes twinkling. 'Oh, he's an android? No wonder the Agency sent him along. So much more predictable and dependable than organics when correcting problematic timelines.' He frowned. 'If I'd realised he was programmed for revenge I would never have agreed to bring him here.'

She gritted her teeth. 'Can you reprogram him, though?'

'Most certainly, I can!'

She cast a weary eye at the vortex manipulator. Twelve minutes left. Another time-distortion-flagged job had appeared since she last checked. Doom knew she had to take it; had to grab every possible chance to find her Doctor.

The Doctor eventually moved away from Stalgon, a device that resembled what Ol Blue Eyes had called a "sonic screwdriver" still in his hand. 'Done!'

Mandroid-Stalgon rose to its feet and peered at Doom as if momentarily befuddled.

Nine minutes. Just enough. Doom knew she couldn't leave without talking to this Doctor. 'Doctor, I'm going. But before I do—'

'Please, you mustn't leave yet. Vassta still needs you.'

She pocketed the monocle tracker, nonchalant. 'Yeah, mate, but I'm on the clock.'

'Tsk, tsk,' he reminded her gravely. 'When in doubt, always choose to help. Now, Stalgon, would you be good enough to reactivate the elevator?'

The android placed a palm over the control panel. After a second, the doors opened.

She offered a hand. 'All right, Stal? Friends?'

The android ignored her.

'You may no longer be his target,' the Doctor began apologetically. 'But turning the android into a friend is considerably more involved, and you did mention that time is short.'

'Yep. It's pretty short.'

'Incidentally, you'll be relieved to hear that the broadcast worked,' the Doctor announced, as they marched abreast through the conference centre. 'The whole planet saw the Raxacoricofallapatorian emerge from the skin of the queen.'

'And did it stop the fighting?'

Evenly, the Doctor replied, 'It did not.'

'Let me do my shocked gasp of surprise,' said Doom.

'"Against stupidity the gods themselves contend in vain,"' murmured the Doctor.

They were close enough to the conference centre to hear the continued pandemonium. Uniformed security guards were still bracing the doors, despite non-stop cries and begging from people inside to be allowed out. Doom dreaded to imagine what they'd find inside.

Mandroid-Stalgon went straight for the guards, picked them up and one by one, hurled them across the corridor. Indignant Raxacoricofallapatorians emerged from the Vasstans' skins. Doom stasered each in turn, using a powerful stun. They probably deserved to die but she was a knight-assassin, not a soldier.

The android threw open the doors. Over the entire hall, an instant silence fell. Dazed Vasstans, many of them smeared with blood and nursing wounded heads, arms and legs, began to limp out, gaping in disgust at the fallen Raxacoricofallapatorians.

Doom watched them stream into the corridor, heart thudding as fury and pity flooded her emotions. 'Arrest D'Mitre and Magdah Tannelo,' she insisted to any Vasstan who'd listen. 'They arranged to assassinate your leaders. This is their fault, too.'

The Doctor gave her a long, thoughtful look. Had he figured out Doom's involvement in this? It didn't matter. She had no problem taking responsibility, especially if it kept the peace. Taking the punishment, that was another matter. She'd been arrested countless times but never done more than a few minutes of jail. The vortex manipulator was handy that way.

As more Vasstans left the hall, the carnage inside became visible. Doom counted fifteen bodies on the floor. Almost everyone else bore some injury. It was astonishing the damage even unarmed people could inflict. Delegates had ripped apart chairs and lamps and used the fragments to beat each other, many to the point of unconsciousness, a few to death.

The Doctor approached a Vasstan man whose arm was being placed in a sling. He had an air of authority and was surrounded by a circle of mostly uninjured people.

Doom spotted the family resemblance at once. This had to be Alexyi's 'Da'. She was about to accuse him when she noticed the Doctor's warning glare. Instead she said, 'We managed to trap the alien that took over Queen Luudmila. She's locked in the upstairs kitchen.'

Lord D'Mitre Tannelo Kadh observed Doom and the Doctor for a moment, appraising them. 'You're the assassin,' he said, nodding at her. 'But you,' he said to the Doctor, 'I don't know.'

'I'm the Doctor.'

'Good. We could use one.'

Doom continued. 'The alien that's locked up is Draja. She's the daughter of Ecktosca, their leader. He's very proud of his daughter, told me this was all her idea. You should use Draja as a bargaining chip.'

D'Mitre nodded. 'Yes. Good.' To the Vasstans surrounding him he said, 'Send the message. Tell Ecktosca that unless he orders the ore suckers to leave Vassta *immediately*, we will execute all aliens and collaborators. His daughter, Draja, we will imprison at the bottom of a very deep, dark hole. No – I have a better idea. We'll hand her over to my wife, the Lady Magdah.'

The attending Vasstans responded with appreciative, rather heartless chuckles, which made Doom feel distinctly iffy.

D'Mitre turned to Doom. 'Now then, you're the one calling for my arrest. Why?'

She pushed out an obstinate chin. 'The Raxacoricofallapatorians may have been behind the plan to use Vassta as an abzantium extraction point. But they couldn't have done it unless people like you and your wife weren't already sowing division.'

'The luxury of hindsight,' D'Mitre said, shrugging. 'When such things begin, it's easy to become swept up. What of you, our chosen instrument, an assassin of the Lesser Order of Oberon? Do you also deserve punishment? Or will you help us to reunite our world?'

Doom swallowed. After so much bloodshed was that even possible?

'Listen, *we* showed your whole world that a Raxacoricofallapatorian impersonated the Kadh queen,' she began. 'And Ecktosca wore the skin of Abo Chenoute to frame him exactly the same way. I saw it. I could tell everyone,' she added hopefully.

D'Mitre considered. 'Very well. Release my wife,' he ordered the nearby Vasstans. 'Bring recording devices – the ones here were all destroyed. Lady Magdah and I will amend publicly for our actions. We will atone through our own reunion. If she and I can agree to honesty and reconciliation, so can all of Vassta.'

From their reactions, Doom gathered that a reunion with Lady Magdah was a scary prospect.

The Doctor and Doom observed for a few moments as D'Mitre began putting his plan in order.

The Doctor turned to face her with an oddly insincere smile. 'What now? Back to killing for the Order?'

'You'd be surprised. Lately I don't seem to need to do much actual killing.'

'Nevertheless.'

'You know, my work *can* be useful,' she challenged. 'Because of me, wars have been avoided.'

The Doctor stuck both hands in his trouser pockets and looked pensive.

She added, tentatively, 'Any chance of a peek at that diary you mentioned?'

'My diary?'

'*His* then, the one before you? I reckon we've met, love to hear his take on it.'

He smiled wryly. 'My dear, what do *you* think?'

'Ohhh, I get it. Back on the whole non-interference thing, are we?'

Sighing, the Doctor shook his head. 'I cannot show you the diary, Doom. I think you know why. But I *can* show you something that will happen approximately two hours from now, here on Vassta. Would you care to see?'

Gruffly she replied, 'Go on, then.'

Lips twitching with humour, from the floor the Doctor picked up a discarded personal communicator. He tweaked it with his sonic device until on its screen, a video began to play.

'I set it to stream from the TARDIS,' he explained. '*This* is what brought me to Vassta, this is the possible future I was shown; that I had to bring about. A preferred future in which a race of terrible creatures *do not* gain control of Vassta's lost abzantium and use it to make their casings practically invincible . . .'

On the device screen, Doom watched the view of the planet from space, its surface deep blue, grey, green and white, all layered beneath a thin swirl of peaceful clouds. There were no longer any vast columns of rocky chunks being pulled into space. The view pulled back further to reveal the departing ore suckers.

'Vassta is safe, Doom. Because of that, the galaxy is safer, too. Today, you helped.' He paused briefly, then leaned closer and lowered his voice. 'It's not impossible that you might someday be asked to confirm my role in this. I trust I can count on you?'

*Me, vouch for the Doctor?* A sense of pride stirred within Doom, powerful enough to bring a hot tear to her eye. She quickly blinked it away. It was good when her job led to such clearly beneficial outcomes, but she wasn't about to let that influence her too much. In the end it was just another day at work. Some days were better than others and this one was mostly worse. If the last four hours seemed to add up to *something* good, maybe she could allow herself a brief moment of satisfaction?

The Doctor shuffled to his feet and pulled back the sleeve of her holosuit to reveal the vortex manipulator. 'Three minutes left, is it? You've just enough time for you to record your testimony. I'll pop back to the TARDIS before mine. Until next time, Miz Doom.'

Doom lowered her eyes to the vortex manipulator, one finger over the new, flagged job. 'Yeah, maybe see you in an hour or so? Not *you* you, another you.'

With one last, enigmatic grin, he was gone.

Her time on Vassta was almost over. Alternatively, she could stay here awhile, squirrel herself away in a deluxe hotel beside a blue lake and tackle a few jigsaw puzzles. Or just a hotel, or just a lake.

*Or just the jigsaw.*

Then she remembered how Death had last appeared to her, not even during an assignment but in the bathroom of a coffee shop on Earth, 2006. It might happen that way again – any time and where she least expected it. Doom could rest or she could devote every remaining second to reversing the collapse of her timeline.

*I'm a walking irony: a time traveller running out of time.*